A Kiss at Christmas

Copyright © 2019 by Meg Easton

All rights reserved.

No part of this book may be reproduced in any form or by any electronic or mechanical means, including information storage and retrieval systems, without written permission from the author, except for the use of brief quotations in a book review.

This is a work of fiction and names, characters, incidents, and places are products of the author's imagination or used fictitiously. Any resemblance to persons, living or dead, incidents, and places is coincidental.

Cover Illustration: Blue Water Books

Interior design: Mountain Heights Publishing

Author website: www.megeaston.com

A Mountain Springs Christmas

The Christmas Pact

The Christmas Bet

The Christmas Clause

Love Started Romances

It Started with a Sunset

It Started with a Note

It Started with a Glance

Silver Leaf Falls romance

Coming Home to Silver Leaf Falls

A Kiss at Christmas

A Kiss at Christmas

MEG EASTON

For my son, Cory

One

KELLI

KELLI ELLIS DROVE her car into Building C's parking lot and saw over the piles of freshly plowed snow that her favorite spot was available.

"Yes!" she shouted to her empty car, "I got here first!" She immediately looked around, sure that Parker Brockbank from Trade Shows was already in the lot, ready to steal it from her. But there wasn't anyone else.

Then, just as she was almost to it, Parker drove in from the opening at the other end of the lot and pulled into her parking spot. The spot that so perfectly had the boughs of a big Ponderosa Pine sticking straight out above it, completely shading the entire parking space in the summer and keeping the snow off her car in the winter.

She shook a fist at Parker's car, pretty sure he was chuckling at having snuck in and grabbed the space when she was so close. Then she went to her second choice spot—C15, which wasn't anything special at all. She looked up just in time to see Parker as he strode down the sidewalk toward the building, looking infuriatingly perfect in his slacks, overcoat, and perfectly imperfect hair.

After grabbing her bag and exiting the car, she checked, and yep—she was evenly spaced between the lines and exactly straight. Unlike Parker's car, which was a good six inches closer to the line at the front than it was at the back.

She had woken up still in a sour mood from the bomb her dad had dropped on her when he and his new wife had stopped by her house last night. But she was determined not to let that, or Parker stealing her spot, ruin her day. She had put on her favorite pair of heels, a pink blousy top, a navy skirt, and the necklace that never failed to get her compliments.

She pushed away the negative thoughts, purposely put a spring in her step, and reminded herself how much she loved her job as she used her keycard to open the front door of the ZentCube offices. After taking the stairs to the second floor, which housed the entire marketing department, she sat at her desk and pretended she had been the first in the office.

It wasn't easy to arrive first—or the second—at the office, but it was worth it. Her constant goal was to be the perfect employee, so getting in early was important. It was when she came up with her best ideas. And when she made the effort to get them, she didn't have to rely on something coming to mind on the fly during marketing meetings—she had ideas, plans, and proposals waiting in the wings.

She smiled at the adorable little Christmas tree on her

desk, straightened her papers and pens, made sure her keyboard was perfectly straight, and then got to work.

At eight-forty, when the first of her coworkers stepped foot on the second floor, she was putting the finishing touches on her ideas for their new advertising campaign. Five minutes later, she went into the break room and grabbed a cup of coffee. She had just taken the first step out of the break room when she heard Parker's boss say to him, "Two o'clock on Wednesday works for Adrian, and I'm guessing it will for the others. Will you get the conference room scheduled?"

Kelli ducked behind a cubicle and pulled out her phone. After opening her email app, she quickly typed an email to Greg, asking if she could schedule the conference room for two on Wednesday, then sent the email before Parker and his boss even finished talking. She chuckled all the way back to her desk, already imagining the look on Parker's face when he realized it was payback for stealing her parking space.

Valeria, her best friend and normally on-time coworker, didn't arrive until ten after nine. She blew into their team's quadrant like a snowstorm, ushering in a rush of air and a flurry of excitement with her.

"Good morning, Sunshine," Kelli said. "You're rather happy today."

Valeria collapsed into her chair at the desk kitty-corner from Kelli's with a sigh. "It was a really good morning. I thought I was going to be here early, but then Rhett—"

Kelli slapped her hands over her ears. "La la la! What's

the rule about being late?" She took her hands off her ears when it was clear Valeria wasn't going to finish her sentence.

Her friend let out a huff of air. "That I can't tell you why if it involves something Rhett and I did until we've been married for at least six months. Preferably twelve." She grabbed the poofy fluff ball that they usually tossed back and forth when they were brainstorming and threw it at Kelli. "I'll tell you what the real solution is, though—Oh. You didn't have so great of a morning, did you?"

"Parker Brockbank in Trade Shows stole my spot, so that wasn't great." Kelli threw the poof ball back and turned to her computer. "But I came up with some great ad copy for the Business Success magazine campaign." Her boss, Liz, was sure to be impressed. Kelli didn't need promotions, the corner office, or a fancy title. What she did need was for her boss, Liz, to be impressed. To see her as a valuable member of the team.

An email notification popped up on her screen and she quickly clicked on it when she saw it was a response from Greg, and she grinned. "I heard that Parker wanted the conference room tomorrow at two, so I emailed Greg right then and it looks like I got it. He even said, 'You emailed just in time, too. Someone requested it less than a minute after you did.'"

Valeria laughed and gave her a high five. "That's my girl." But she'd been studying Kelli the whole time she'd been talking. "Okay, today's good. It was last night, then, that was bad."

"How do you always know?"

Valeria smiled and threw the poof back to her. "If I say what your tell is, then you'll stop doing it. Now, about last night. Spill."

"My dad came over."

"Oh, good. I know you've been feeling like you haven't seen him enough lately." Then Valeria's face dropped. "Oh. He brought the evil stepmother with him."

"JoAnn isn't evil. She's just..." Kelli wanted to end the sentence with, "a thief who stole my dad," but she was trying to be an adult about this. "She just wants to work on blending the newly combined family."

"A family that she doesn't want you to be a part of."

Kelli nodded but didn't let herself think of it fully. She wasn't about to let the door open on that much pain—no one needed to know how much it hurt her. Not even Valeria.

"What happened?"

"Well, my dad texted to ask if he could bring me over a couple of éclairs from Petrocelli's. I should've known right then and there that he was buttering me up. He didn't tell me that he was bringing JoAnn with him—that was a surprise I got to enjoy when I opened the door, threw my arms around my dad's neck, and saw her standing there.

"So they come in, sit down in my living room, and my dad awkwardly hands me the pastry box. Then he and JoAnn look at each other, and I can see that my dad is nervous, but JoAnn gives him an encouraging smile. So he starts talking about how this is the first Christmas they are celebrating since getting married and about how difficult it is to bring two separate families into one and all that. So they decided that for Christmas, it might be best to do that in isolation and get away to have some bonding time."

"So..." Valeria said, "he wants you to go hang out with him and JoAnn and your three new stepsisters over Christmas at some secluded cabin in the mountains? Like with no escape?"

"Honest to goodness, that's right where my mind went, too. And I was wondering if I could get along with three teenagers who want nothing to do with me and want every second of my dad's attention. But no. Instead of a cabin in the mountains, it's a beach resort in Cabo San Lucas. And when he said they needed to bring two separate families together for bonding, they meant my dad and JoAnn's daughters."

"They didn't invite you?" Valeria's voice was every bit as incredulous as she needed it to be. It was one of the reasons why she made the best friend ever.

"Nope. My dad tried to sell it by saying how awesome it would be for me to celebrate Christmas with him early and to have some one-on-one time. And how much more special it would be to spend all day with him on the twenty-first instead of the entire week of Christmas because the twenty-first happens first. And how great it will be for me to be free to do whatever I want over Christmas break instead of being tied down by family things."

"Please tell me you told him what you really think of that."

"What was I supposed to do, Val? Tell him to cancel the trip?"

"Or tell him to invite you. And to remember that you are every bit as much a part of the family as JoAnn's daughters are."

Kelli shook her head. "It was just me and my dad against the world since I was in eighth grade. I got to hang out with my dad more than most people do. JoAnn's girls are in junior high and high school. They've been without a dad for a few years, and they're desperate for time with mine. Maybe I should just give him up. I mean, I'm twenty-six years old. I shouldn't need to see my daddy all the time anymore."

She didn't even consider mentioning to Val how it had felt like she'd lost the only family she had when her dad got remarried, but she could tell by the look on Valeria's face that she knew it without Kelli saying.

"I know!" Valeria said. "Come spend Christmas with me and Rhett. Spend the week, even. We can pretend we're twelve and having a sleepover."

"In your teeny apartment."

"You can sleep on the couch. Or we'll put an air mattress in that space between the tree and the kitchen."

"Most people call that space a 'hallway.'"

"It'll be cozy."

"Valeria. I appreciate the offer. You know I do. But this is your first Christmas as a newly married couple. I don't want to ruin that for you."

"It'll be fun!"

"Remember how I said I didn't want to hear about your morning with Rhett?"

"Yeah...On second thought, you really don't want to be around us at Christmas."

At the sound of someone loudly clearing their throat, Kelli and Valeria spun in their chairs to see Liz.

"Sorry to interrupt your sleepover plans, but Kelli, do you have the mock-ups for the print ads?"

Of course, Liz had to stop by when she was socializing instead of during any of the time she had been working diligently already today. She turned back to her desk and grabbed the folder that had been leaning against her binders, revealing an upside-down white paper cup that had a picture of a spider drawn on it with the words *Don't lift until you're ready to squash it!*

Kelli screamed and shoved herself away from her desk, her chair rolling backward until it hit something, and then she jumped out of her chair to get more space between the cup and her. "I've been sitting next to that thing for more than two hours?!"

Her heart raced, her breaths were ragged, and it was likely that everyone on the second floor had heard her scream, but right now, she didn't care. All she cared about was that a spider had been crawling around who knew how much of her desk before someone trapped it with that cup, and it had been probably pacing with those spindly legs around that little circle of space on her desk the whole time she'd been working.

And now, all she could think about was how that little stealthy, moving, vial of poison with its shiny or hairy—either was gross—abdomen and its eight beady eyes were right there in that cup, just waiting for its chance to escape and come after her. "Someone kill it!" Her hand was on her chest like she could manually stop her heart from beating so fast and hard.

"Don't worry," Valeria said, "I've got you." She grabbed a notepad and held it level with Kelli's desk right at the edge, then slid the cup onto the notepad. Then she flipped it over and, in a move that made Kelli's heart shudder, Valeria lifted the notepad off and looked inside the cup. She put the hand holding the notepad on her hip and tipped the cup toward Kelli. "There's nothing in it."

Kelli's first thought was that it had escaped and could possibly be on her, but in a flash, she knew there had never been a spider. This was a prank. She looked over the top of her cubicle to the crowd of people that had gathered to see what her scream was about, and she saw Parker Brockbank giving a sly smile big enough to bring out that adorable dimple in his right cheek, a mischievous gleam in his eye. But, at least he had the decency to look contrite before ducking away.

"If you're ever having a sluggish morning where coffee isn't doing the trick," Kelli said to all the coworkers gathered around her cubicle, "and you need a good old-fashioned scream to get the heart pumping, you know where to find me."

They all chuckled as they headed back to their desks, and then Kelli turned to Liz. "I am so sorry. I might have a slight fear of spiders. Um, here are the mock-ups. Let me know what changes you'd like or if you want to meet to discuss."

She tried to make her voice sound extra professional to combat the dose of unprofessionalism she had just shown.

"Thank you. I will."

She thought she caught a slight smile on Liz's face as she was walking away. Great. That's all she wanted—to be the office entertainment.

After pushing her chair back to the vicinity of her desk, she took a moment to shoot a glare in the direction of Parker Brockbank's desk, even though she couldn't see it from hers. Then she sat down and faced her computer, re-straightening everything. "Can you take your lunch hour at one tomorrow and join me for a project?"

"Of course!" Valeria said. "What do you have in mind?"

Kelli started typing an email message. "I'm letting Greg know that I need the conference room at one instead of two, so whoever wanted it at two can have it."

"And what are we doing in there at one?"

"We are spending the hour blowing up balloons and filling the conference room as full of them as we can. Unless..." She turned in her chair to face Valeria. "Do you think Parker has a phobia? Like, of snakes? Maybe we can fill it with plastic snakes instead."

"Whatever it is, I'm in."

That's what she loved about Valeria. She gave her support, even when it meant helping with a prank, and she had fun with every bit of it.

But Kelli wasn't doing this for fun—she was doing it to get even.

Two

PARKER

PARKER HAD BEEN RUNNING behind all day. His days usually consisted of talking to person after person—on his team, in his department, in other parts of the company, and on phone calls outside of the company. So the only time he could get any good planning and research in was if he came in at seven, before everyone else got in.

But this morning before he left for work, his buddy Josh, who was the marketing director at a business training company, had called. He said that they were looking for a brand marketing manager, and they wanted him. Parker hadn't even been looking for another job—especially after Stephanie had pulled the rug out from under him and made him second guess how capable he was at making valuable contributions.

Brand marketing manager had been a job he'd had his eyes on since he'd graduated college, though. The offer had hit him like a snowstorm blowing in. ZentCube was a great company to work for, and he'd be crazy to leave. But the current brand marketing manager at ZentCube would be crazy to leave, too, so the same job here wasn't likely to open anytime soon.

Maybe now was a good time for multiple fresh starts.

As soon as he'd hung up the phone, all Parker had been able to do was think about the job while wandering around his apartment in a possibilities-fueled daze that had been both exciting and exhausting. He had pulled into work more than an hour later than he liked and of course, Kelli Ellis from Digital and Print Marketing had already taken his parking spot.

He smiled thinking about yesterday, though. Who would've thought that a simple paper cup and a Sharpie could've caused such a reaction? Enough of a reaction that he'd felt a little bad about it for a moment.

He knew their pranks were a bit childish, but they'd become almost a tradition at work. They added so much life to the day—like a shot of espresso. They were a bright spot, especially when he'd been going through hard things.

As he was preparing the final mockups for their trade show displays for his two o'clock meeting in the conference room, he thought of Kelli again. When Greg had responded saying that he'd just missed being able to reserve the conference room because someone had requested it a minute earlier, he knew that someone was Kelli. She had been the only other person in the office that early.

And then it suddenly became available moments after she had discovered the spider cup. She was up to something, and he got more and more wary as two o'clock neared. He finished packing up his stuff and headed into the conference room five minutes before he was supposed to meet his boss, the product manager, and a couple of people on his team.

Everything was fine, though. His meeting went great, and they finalized decisions on which mockup to use and what last-minute changes needed to be made. He left the room feeling energized and ready to get started on the changes. He had been second-guessing the direction he'd gone with this coming year's event display and worried that it was the wrong choice entirely, but after that brainstorming session, he knew it was going to be the best they'd ever had.

He was practically whistling his way back to his desk alongside his coworkers, and then he stopped dead in his tracks when his desk came into view. Darren and Hannah stopped too, and then they burst into laughter. They were the first to race forward and check it out. Parker stayed back a bit, unsure if he wanted to see it closer. Then, curiosity got the better of him, and he walked up to it.

His entire cubicle was covered in cat pictures. No—on closer inspection, he saw it was just one cat; the pictures were just taken at all different angles. There were poster-sized cat pictures on the walls of his cubicle, one-inch high pictures completely covering all four sides of the outside frame of his monitor, a framed picture of the cat on his desk, and an *Ode to My Cat* poem on the wall.

On one wall, the one most open to everyone's view, of course, there was a full-length picture of Parker that was a good two feet tall, cut out, with a speech bubble that said, "I love you, Princess Olive." And of course, there was a speech bubble on a picture of the cat that said, "And I am willing to share my space with you, Parker. Most of the time." The cat was wearing a Santa hat.

There were even pictures of the cat—Olive, apparently —covering every inch of his desk, underneath all his papers and office supplies. And little tiny pictures of Olive on the C, the A, and the T letters on his keyboard. In one corner sat a stuffed cat whose back legs were seated but whose front legs were standing tall, looking regal and judgmental, with a Christmas wreath around its neck like a necklace.

He couldn't help it—he burst out laughing. This was good. And so not what he had expected. He turned to Darren. "Did you tell Kelli that I have a cat allergy?"

"It may have come up in conversation."

He shook his head and then pulled his phone out of his pocket when it started buzzing. Seeing it was his mom, he said, "You'll have to excuse me," to Darren and Hannah and then answered it as they both walked back to their cubicles.

"Hi, Mom."

"Hi, Sweetie. Is this a bad time? I hate bothering you at work—"

"It's totally fine, Mom. If it was a problem, I wouldn't have answered. You know you can call anytime."

"You're a good son, you know? Okay, so today is the last day that your dad and I can cancel our cruise reservations without penalty and—"

"Don't cancel, Mom. This is your thirtieth anniversary. You guys deserve to go live it up to celebrate."

"I know. It's just that it's over Christmas."

"You love having your anniversary on Christmas Eve, and you should get to go on your anniversary trip during your anniversary."

Truthfully, Parker was going to miss them. Christmas Eve at home always consisted of celebrating his parents' anniversary with a feast, followed by making gingerbread dream homes, then bundling up and going caroling as a family. It was going to feel wrong to not do that.

Until this year, Christmas was one holiday that he looked forward to as an adult every bit as much as he had when he was a kid. But ever since Stephanie broke off their engagement, he'd lost all desire to celebrate Christmas at all. The magic it held was just gone. Still, though, he was going to miss it this year. But it wasn't like he was going to have his parents skip the trip they had been planning practically his whole life.

"I don't know if it's right to leave."

Parker twirled his pen, which now had a little eraser pushed on the top—like they used in elementary school—in the shape of a cat. Of course, it did. "Ethan is fine to spend Christmas with the Garlands at their cabin?"

Parker's boss Adam walked over to his desk, some of the sketches from their meeting in his hand. Parker held up a finger, motioning for him to wait a moment.

"He's thrilled about it. It's on a lake, so he'll be in heaven the whole time and we'll be lucky if he even stops to think about us once."

"Then it's right for you two to go."

"It's *you* I'm worried about, honey."

"If your fourteen-year-old son is fine with it, I think it's safe to assume that your twenty-seven-year-old son is okay with it, too."

"I never would've planned it if I hadn't truly believed you'd be spending Christmas honeymooning it up on your own cruise."

He tried not to feel the stab of pain at her mention of how different his life should be right now. "I really will be fine if you go. I will find a way to celebrate Christmas on my own."

It was a lie—he hadn't planned on celebrating at all. But he didn't lie to his mom, and the guilt hit him instantly. He vowed to listen to a Christmas song, or get a foot-and-a-half tall Christmas tree like Kelli had on her desk and put it up in his apartment. Some little thing that could be considered "celebrating Christmas" so it wasn't a lie.

"You will?"

"I will."

"Okay, then, we'll keep our trip. But if you change your mind, even last minute, you let me know and we'll cancel and take the penalty."

"I will. But don't worry—I'm not going to change my mind."

"I love you, son."

"I love you, too, Mom."

Parker hung up the phone and turned to Adam, motioning at the papers in his hand. "More thoughts?"

"Oh, yeah." Adam looked down at the papers for a moment, like he'd forgotten he was holding them. "I was thinking about this section here, where it says, 'higher,' the display should physically go higher." Then he turned his attention from the papers back to Parker. "You don't have anywhere to go for Christmas?"

Parker shook his head. "Not really, but who knows? I might spend the holiday with friends." Not a lie, because he didn't say he was—just that he *might*. If all his friends weren't either married or going home to their parents for Christmas, or both, which he was pretty sure they all were. "How much higher are you thinking? Subtle, or aim-for-the-ceiling?"

Adam dropped the hand holding the plans to his side. "Come to my house for Christmas. Erin and the kids would love it. You can have a Christmas Eve feast with us, and watch Luke and Holly be Mary and Joseph, with Holly holding her baby doll, and a bunch of their stuffed animals playing the part of the stable animals. It'll be unpredictable in the way only a two-year-old and a four-year-old can make it.

"We've got a guest room. We'll open presents on Christmas morning, you can see how great it is to experience the magic of Christmas through the eyes of little kids, and we'll eat warm cinnamon rolls for breakfast. It'll be great. What do you say?"

It would be great. It was exactly what Parker wanted. His

breakup with Stephanie had been difficult all along but especially right now, since they were supposed to get married the week of Christmas. The last thing he needed was to hang out with a guy who had everything Parker wanted, at a time when he was acutely aware of how much he didn't have it. Especially when it was just a pity ask. His boss didn't really want him there.

"I'll think about it and let you know. Show me what you were thinking about that display."

Adam studied him for a moment, and by the look on the guy's face, he knew Parker's promise to think about it was just a way to stall him until he told him no. He lifted the papers he had been holding so they both could see and discuss them.

Parker just needed to accept that the magic of Christmas was just a childhood thing that he should've grown out of. The magic was gone, along with any need to celebrate this year. He was fine spending it alone.

Three

KELLI

As soon as Kelli heard voices mid-conversation as the conference room door opened, she grabbed her tape dispenser and the few random cat pictures that they hadn't yet found a place for, and she and Valeria ducked into the break room before Parker and his team rounded the corner. They peeked through the one window that had a perfect view of Parker's desk and waited.

"I think you should start dating again," Valeria whispered.

"What?" The randomness of the comment caught her off guard.

"You know, get back on the horse again. They say the longer you wait, the more you'll fear getting bucked off again."

"It's not the right time."

"It's been a year since you and James broke up. It's time."

She was very sure it wasn't time. One of the hardest things about the break-up had been with James's family. She had fit in with them, and could even see where her place was in his family. Breaking up with James meant breaking up with his family. And now that her own little family of two—she and her dad—were doing their own kind of breaking apart, she couldn't expose herself to that possibility again with someone else.

It wasn't until months after she and James had stopped dating that she realized she'd fallen for him because she'd wanted a family so badly, and his was so great. She didn't trust herself to date anyone right now for fear that she'd make the same mistake again.

Especially because, right now, she desperately wanted a family. For the first time, she hated that ZentCube gave them nearly two weeks off for Christmas and New Year's. It was a long time to be alone and feel like she didn't belong anywhere. This year, she was dreading the break.

Yeah. It was definitely not the time to start dating. It would surely be a mistake.

"Shh! They're coming!"

She held her breath as Parker came into view and wished more than anything that from this angle they could see his face and not just his backside. Parker froze when he saw their handiwork, and Darren and Hannah raced forward to look at it closer.

Parker's dress shirt was fitted enough that she could see his back muscles perfectly, so Kelli watched them closely, along with his arms and hands. But not so that she could admire them—she'd stopped herself from doing that long ago. And then stopped herself again every day, just like she stopped herself now. No, this time she watched so she could interpret his reaction.

The muscles in his shoulders twitched and his arms were rigid. She chuckled. He looked properly annoyed. Score one for team Kelli and Valeria.

Then Parker *laughed*. A big, hearty laugh. That was unexpected. And, surprisingly, it made her feel like she'd won this particular battle in their "Let's see who can annoy the other person more" war. Interesting.

He walked forward to check out their display of cat affection, which was pretty great if she did say so herself. She knew he was seconds from turning around to see if he could see the person who had done it—like he'd guess it would be anyone other than Kelli—so she said, "We better get out of here."

Instead of walking out the door on their usual side, they took the door on the opposite side of the break room and walked the long way around, so Parker wouldn't see them. She chuckled the whole way.

They had almost made it back to their desks when her phone buzzed with a notification. She looked at the screen, eyebrows scrunched together, while she tried to make sense of what she was seeing.

"What is it?"

Kelli held the phone so Valeria could read it.

"Carla Cook... Isn't she the assistant to one of the bigwigs?"

Kelli nodded and opened the text with a shaking finger and read the message out loud. "'Hello, Kelli. Merit Casselman and Graham McNeil would like to meet with you today at three-thirty in Building HQ, on the third floor. Please let me know if you'll be able to make this meeting time.' Why do the CEO and the CTO want to meet with me?" She glanced back in the direction of Parker's desk. "Do you think I'm in trouble for the cat prank?"

"How would they even know about that? Besides, it's not exactly something you'd get called on the carpet for."

But Kelli's stomach had already fallen, her ears were on fire, and she was feeling very lightheaded. "I don't know. It's got to be something." Her mind raced, trying to figure out what she could be in trouble for. Wouldn't they just have her boss talk to her if she wasn't doing something right? Or maybe even someone from Human Resources? Why in the world would the two co-founders of the company need to see her?

She looked at Valeria. "Did you get a message?"

Just as they reached their desks, Valeria picked up the phone that she'd left behind. "Nope. No emails or texts at all. Maybe it's for something good."

"You don't get called to the third floor of headquarters for something good."

Valeria glanced at her watch. "Well, you've got twenty-two minutes until you need to be there. What can we work on that will take your mind off of it for a few minutes?"

"Nothing." Kelli shook her head. "I think maybe I should just head over there now."

Getting there early had been a mistake. A winter snowstorm was just rolling in, and big, fat snowflakes were covering her coat and hood by the time she'd walked three buildings over to headquarters.

She stomped her feet in the lobby, shook the snow off her coat, and then took the elevator to the third floor. She had seen Merit Casselman quite a few times over the two-and-a-half years that she'd worked at ZentCube, and had met Graham several times, too, but she had never been to the third floor before.

The receptionist on the third floor led her to Carla, who directed her to a seat outside of Merit's office, facing a Christmas tree she couldn't even focus on, to wait for him to finish the meeting he was in. The walk hadn't helped to calm her racing heart. The cold air hadn't cleared the lightheadedness. Forcing herself to do calm breathing as she sat and waited didn't stop her leg from bouncing.

And nothing stopped her from feeling like she was sitting outside the principal's office, about to find out exactly how much trouble she was in.

Finally, at three-thirty-two, the door opened, and Kelli stood. The two head honchos were shaking someone's hand and talking in happy voices to him, but Kelli's brain was so full of worries that she hadn't thought to notice if the guy was wearing a ZentCube employee badge or not. As the man was walking away, Graham turned to Kelli. "Welcome, Miss Ellis. Please, come in."

She shook both of their hands and then swallowed as she walked into the office. Instead of sitting down across the very large desk from them, as she had imagined, Merit motioned to a seating area in the other half of the office, where two chairs and a couch were arranged around a coffee table.

Not knowing which seat to take, she sat in the closest one—a padded armchair—and wiped her hands on her slacks, straightening them while also making her hands less clammy.

Graham sat down in the other armchair and Merit sat in the middle of the couch, his arms spread wide on the back of the couch, looking about a million times more comfortable than she felt. Of course, he wasn't the one being called in to talk to the big boss.

"Every year," Graham said, "we take about a dozen employees on a Christmas retreat. Have you ever heard anyone talk about it?"

Kelli shook her head. Should she have? Or was it something she wasn't supposed to hear about?

"Every year it's a little different, but we always go to our managers and ask if they know of anyone on their teams who doesn't have a place to go for Christmas. Then we take a look, narrow down the list as needed, and form a group."

They wouldn't be smiling so much and chatting about fancy retreats if she was in a lot of trouble, right? So maybe they wanted her to do something? Like, make some kind of marketing materials for the retreat? It was weird they were coming to her directly instead of going to her boss or the marketing director, but she could do that. Or should she already have been doing that and she somehow missed the message that she was supposed to?

"We've gone several different places in the past," Merit added. "But during the summer, Graham sent me to The Royal Palms resort in Myrtle Beach, South Carolina, and it was amazing."

Graham chuckled. "And he's not just saying that because he met the love of his life, Elise, while he was there."

Merit grinned, and Kelli saw a hint of a blush. This was all great, but she still didn't understand why she was here, in Merit's office. She wanted to run her sweaty palms across her slacks again, but she was trying to be professional, but it left her not having a clue what to do with her hands. So she just set them beside her legs on the seat.

"I've been there, too," Graham said, "and I think it's a perfect place for our retreat. We want to take a group there this Christmas, especially, because Elise is over all the Christmas events. And since Merit and I do this thing together, I think I might be on my own if I took us somewhere other than where Elise is."

The two of them were smiling like kids at Christmas, but Kelli still didn't get why she was even in on this conversation.

"So," she asked, "are you wanting me to do some kind of pamphlets for it, or come up with some images to—"

Merit laughed and interrupted. "No, we want you to come!"

"You... What?" She looked at both of them, trying to make sense of the words. "I don't understand. You want me to work at the retreat?"

Graham chuckled, shaking his head. "The first year we did this, ZentCube was probably one-tenth the size it is now and we were all in the same building. We found out that a few people had nowhere to go for Christmas, so we decided to do something about it. We know it can be hard around the holidays to not be with family, and we know how much fun it can be to spend it with a group of people that you may or may not know.

"And this year, we'd like you to join us. *As a guest*. And don't worry—we pay for everything. Will you come?"

She gasped as their words finally sank in, a lightness filling her chest and making it seem like she was floating right out of her chair. Were they really inviting her to go on vacation? And giving her a place to go for Christmas so she wouldn't be alone? "For real?"

"For real," Merit said.

Kelli's heart practically burst out of her chest with so much happiness and gratitude that it made her jump out of her chair and hug Graham, and then go around the little table and hug Merit. "Yes! Yes, I want to go!"

She was going to have a place to go for Christmas. It was all she could do to not let happy tears spill down her cheeks right in front of the company's founders. When they led her out of the room to pick up a packet of information from

Carla, she hugged it tight to her chest. She kept hugging it tight as she put on her coat and speed-walked back to her building, not even caring that she was getting covered in snow.

She wasn't going to be alone. She was going to belong somewhere.

Four

PARKER

PARKER WORKED on putting in the last of the design element's changes so he could get them finalized and sent to the trade show exhibit company they used before the end of the day, running his mouse over the cat-themed mouse pad his desk now had.

Darren's chair creaked as it turned around behind Parker, just before he heard his teammate and friend say, "So, I see you haven't taken the cats down yet."

"Well, you know me. I *love* cats." Kelli—and probably Valeria, he was guessing—had put a lot of effort into this. It would be a shame to waste such hard work. A prank as good as this one deserved to stick around for a few days. He tweaked the dimensions on the plans a bit until they looked perfect.

"I don't think it's the cat that you're so fond of."

"Ha ha," Parker said without even turning around.

"I think you're fond of the girl who put it up."

"Kelli?"

"Obviously."

Parker shook his head. "We just like to annoy each other. Like you're doing with me right now."

He clicked save on the plans and then sent a message to his boss. *All done. Take a look?*

Darren didn't respond, but he also didn't hear his coworker's chair turn back to his desk, so Parker turned around in his chair to face him.

"I'm just saying that deep down, I think you want to ask her on a date."

"Darren, I *just* got out of a serious relationship."

The guy shook his head. "Nope. That was over two months ago. It's time."

"Who says that two months is the standard amount of time to get over an engagement and move on?"

"Dude. There's no standard. It's different for every person and for every relationship. I'm telling you that for you, with that breakup, it's time." Darren stood up and walked over to Parker's desk, leaning against the framework of his cubicle.

Parker turned back around in his chair to face his computer screen. "And I think you don't have any idea what you're talking about."

"We all know why you do the initial spiel at trade shows. I mean, you've got that face that's all symmetrical and that deep voice. People like listening to people with pretty faces. Now tell me why they have me talk to the ones who are interested in learning more."

"Because even when people tell you they're not interested, you won't stop bugging them about it?"

Parker barely caught sight of the stuffed cat as it flew toward him, and barely turned in time to catch it.

"No, pretty boy. It's because I'm good at reading people." He caught the cat that Parker threw at him and then pointed at him with it. "And I'm telling you that you're ready to date again, whether you think you are or not. Ask her out already."

"We already went out."

The look on Darren's face was comical. A mix of shock and surprise and disbelief. Apparently, he wasn't good at reading everything.

Darren grabbed his chair and pulled it across the aisle and sat down facing Parker. "When? Why did you not tell me about this?"

"Relax, Darren. It was like two-and-a-half years ago. Right after I first started working here."

"What happened? How did it go?"

Parker let out a breath of a laugh, shaking his head. So much of that date had been awkward. "Not well. My aunt Aftyn bumped into us at the restaurant and asked, 'Aww! Is this the girl you were telling me all about? I'm so happy to see you together. No, wait. The girl you told me about had brown hair... Why aren't you dating her anymore?'"

"You're making that up."

"I swear to you I'm not. And then as I'm paying for dinner, my card gets declined. If that wasn't embarrassing enough, the next one gets declined, too—apparently, there was some fraudulent activity on my account and they were 'protecting me'—and I didn't have enough cash to cover the meal.

"So she paid. Luckily I had bought the movie tickets online in advance. Although it probably would've been better if I hadn't, because she got sick from something at dinner, and I couldn't even take her home because my mind had still been back on why my cards had been declined, so I locked my keys in the car."

Darren shook his head.

"Let's just say it was a bad enough first date to convince us both it wasn't meant to be and guarantee we'd never have a second date. And then I started dating Stephanie and we got engaged and she went on to almost get engaged to James."

"Shut up. So, wait. Is that why you two started pranking each other? Because you had an awkwardly embarrassing first date, which made working on the same floor with each other awkward, so that was a way to turn the focus off the date and onto something else?"

Huh. He'd never really thought of it that way before. Maybe Darren could read people better than he'd given him credit for.

"You can't tell me that you'd let a little thing like an awkward first date *two-and-a-half years ago* stop you from asking someone out who you very clearly have chemistry with."

Parker shook his head. "It's not just because of a bad date. I'd never be good enough for someone like her."

Darren's head jerked back in surprise. "Are you being real right now?"

Parker didn't even bother answering. If Darren knew everything that was on the list Stephanie had given him when she broke off their engagement that detailed all the ways in which Parker was deficient, he wouldn't be questioning it at all.

"You used to own every room you walked into, Parker. You used to have the confidence to ask any woman out. What did Stephanie do to you?"

Parker was spared having to answer when his computer chimed its email alert. He turned to it and opened the email.

"I really think you should talk about this," Darren said.

Like that was going to happen. Parker stood up and grabbed his coat from the hook on his cubicle. "Maybe some other time, buddy. It looks like I have a meeting at HQ right now."

"At HQ? Why do you have a meeting at headquarters?"

"You got me," Parker called out as he headed toward the elevators. "Whatever it is, wish me luck!"

It was nearly five, and it was already getting dark outside. All of the streetlights were on in the parking lots of the buildings as he walked toward headquarters, the falling snow lit up in the rays of light below each one. He stepped into the building at the top of ZentCube's campus, stomped off his shoes, shook his coat, and brushed the snowflakes out of his hair before heading to the elevator.

When he reached the third floor, the receptionist took him to Merit Casselman's assistant, Carla. She thanked him for coming, then led him to Merit's office and poked her head in the door. "Parker Brockbank is here. He's your last appointment of the day." Then she opened the door the rest of the way, motioned for him to go inside, then left and shut the door behind her.

The office was nice. Good furniture, not overly decorated. He had met both Merit and Graham several times. He'd even chatted with Graham for quite a while at last year's Christmas party. They had both been sitting on the armrests of a chair and a couch, chatting, but stood when he walked in.

"Parker," Graham said as he shook his hand, "thanks for coming to meet with us. Have a seat."

Parker shook Merit's hand, too, and then sat down in the one seat that neither of them had been leaning against when he walked in. The two of them sat, too.

"It's been a long day," Merit said, "and we know you probably want to get home, so we won't beat around the bush. We've heard you don't have anywhere to go for Christmas."

Ouch. Not only was it a reminder of the broken engagement, but also that he wasn't going to have any family around.

"And we want to change that."

Parker raised an eyebrow.

Graham looked at Merit, laughing. "Well, that definitely couldn't be called 'beating around the bush,' that's for sure." Then he turned to Parker. "You'll have to forgive us. You're our twelfth and last meeting of the day, and I think we peaked in our delivery of this message somewhere around the third or fourth person."

"Maybe you should've made a slideshow," Merit said.

"A slideshow! I can't believe I didn't think of that! Ah, well. It's too late now, so we'll just spell it out. Every year, we have a Christmas celebration with a group of employees who don't have family around to celebrate with."

"And this year," Merit said, "we are doing it at a resort on the coast in South Carolina. A week-long, all expenses paid. Twelve employees—"

"Assuming you tell us yes," Graham cut in.

"—plus me and Graham for most of it. We'd love to have you join us."

The shock made Parker lean back in his chair. "Wow. That's incredible. Really."

"Is that a yes?" Graham asked.

A week-long vacation at a beach resort with a dozen coworkers, or home alone in his apartment with a foot or two of snow. The two didn't compare at all. If he stayed here, he'd be surrounded by people who wanted to celebrate Christmas, when he just wanted to skip it this year. If he was on a beach where there was no snow, it wouldn't even feel like Christmas.

And if all the people going didn't have anyone to spend Christmas with, either, they likely were just as opposed to celebrating as he was. It sounded like a perfect way to get away from it all and pretend like the holiday wasn't even happening.

But how could he say yes to ZentCube paying to fly him across the country to a resort on the beach when he had a job offer on the table that he hadn't decided about yet? It was a really good position with good pay. How could he accept this trip, and then quit the company right after? The guilt was already creeping in.

Sure, he could decide to stay at ZentCube, but there was no guarantee of that. Saying yes would be a jerk move. He wasn't a jerk, so obviously he couldn't accept.

"I'm sorry. I can't."

Both Merit's and Graham's faces fell.

"You really can't?" Graham asked. "Why?"

Maybe he was a jerk after all—the guy looked crushed. He tried to grasp a reason that wouldn't be lying but would explain why he couldn't go, but everything he came up with sounded flimsy. An excuse that would only add insult to their offer. Like he was going to turn his nose up at their big plans because he needed to water his houseplants or something.

He ran his hands over his face. There was nothing he could say that wasn't going to offend, so he might as well tell the entire truth. Then he could at least live with himself.

"I got a job offer at another company."

"Oh," Merit said.

"Not that I was looking! A buddy of mine just contacted me and said his company wants me as their Brand Manager."

Merit's eyes were still on him. "And you told them yes?"

Parker shook his head. "I haven't decided yet—they just asked yesterday. I have to let him know by the first of the year."

The room was silent for several long, excruciating moments while the two leaders of ZentCube pondered and looked at each other, giving nothing away in their expressions. Did he just commit career suicide with this company? Maybe he'd be walking out of this office with termination papers in hand.

Then Graham leaned forward, his forearms resting on his knees, hands clasped in front of him. "Come with us over Christmas."

Parker's eyebrows shot up. But still, he shook his head. "I can't. Because then if I decided to take the other job—well, I wouldn't be okay with the kind of person that would make me."

"Think of it this way," Merit said. "Did you play any sports in high school?"

Parker nodded. "Baseball."

"Any colleges try to recruit you?"

"Two."

"The recruiters—did they wine and dine you to convince you to go to their school?"

Parker smiled at the memory. It had felt pretty cool as a kid who had so little of life figured out. "They did."

Merit leaned forward, nearly matching Graham's pose. "Then pretend this is the same thing. We're trying to recruit you to stay on here. If, after the retreat's over, you decide to leave, then no hard feelings. We'll rest easy knowing we tried our best, and you'll know you made the decision that's best for your career path. Deal?"

Being able to spend the week of Christmas away from Christmas. Not only did that sound more heavenly than his younger self ever would've guessed, but it might also put him in a better mind frame to make the decision. And if Merit and Graham both knew where he stood going into the trip, he wouldn't have to feel guilty about it.

He looked at both men for a long moment. Then he said, "Okay, I'm in."

Merit and Graham both grinned big, shook his hand, and gave him slaps on the back before sending him out to Carla to pick up a packet with the trip details.

As he walked back out into the snow, he released the burden of Christmas that he hadn't realized had been so heavy until he experienced how light he felt without it. The thought of skipping Christmas brought a big smile to his face. This was going to be perfect.

Five

KELLI

KELLI PUSHED her rolling suitcase as the line for airport security inched forward, and then opened Valeria's text that had just popped up on her phone.

Kelli smiled and typed back *Pinkie promise.*

She pushed her suitcase around the switchback in the fabric barrier and then typed her response.

> VALERIA: Kels. These are all people who have no one to spend Christmas with, so they are likely all SINGLE. Cozy up to one of them. It'll be good for you.

She was scrolling through the facial expressions emojis to find one that perfectly encapsulated what she thought of Valeria's comment and glanced up to see how close to the front of the line she was getting. Only about eight more people in front of her. Then she noticed who had just gone through airport security. She abandoned her emoji search and instead typed a message.

> KELLI: You are never going to believe who just went through airport security!

> VALERIA: Who?

> KELLI: Parker Brockbank from Trade Shows! What do you think he's doing here?

She pulled her ID out of the pocket of her shoulder bag and opened her phone to the boarding pass. A notification at the top of the screen popped up with Valeria's response.

> VALERIA: Well, if I had to guess, I'd say he's looking to get on a plane.

> KELLI: Ha ha.

> VALERIA: He's probably going home for Christmas.

> Oh, hey, Christina Jensen in SEO is
> flying home today, too. If you see her, tell
> her I said hi.

Of course. Parker was probably flying home for Christmas. This was the first day they were off work for the holidays, so it made total sense.

Kelli handed her ID to the TSA agent and then put her phone on the scanner to have it read her boarding pass. The agent let her through, and she entered the screening line across from the line Parker was in. He had just removed his laptop and placed everything on the conveyor belt. He was so wrapped up in what he was doing that he hadn't even noticed her. So she just watched him as she waited.

Because really, he was a very attractive guy. She rarely let herself admire him because then her stomach would get all fluttery and then she'd have to remind herself how awkward their first date was years ago and how obviously unsuited they were for each other, and that was usually all she needed to stop.

On the rare occasion that didn't work, she'd remind herself about the time a month or two later when she had first started dating James, and she had ducked out of work in the middle of the day to have a super sweet phone call with him in the print and copy room.

They had been talking for much longer than Kelli had guessed they would, and Parker had come into the room not long before they hung up. When she turned around, Parker chided her for taking personal calls on company time.

Only a few weeks after that, she went into the break room to grab a soda to hopefully help her wake up from a late-afternoon slump, and she caught him making out with his girlfriend before she was even his fiancée. Remembering what a hypocrite he was helped, too.

She was just putting her stuff onto the moving belt when Parker went through the scanner. When he stepped through, the security officer stopped him, but she wasn't close enough to hear what he said and had to turn her focus to getting her own things through security. She wasn't stopped at all, and couldn't help but give him a smirk as he was being patted down and having his fingers tested for bomb residue while she strolled to her bags and grabbed her things.

"Have a great Christmas!" she called out to him as she pulled her rolling bag behind her, grinning all the way to her gate.

She had barely found a seat, hooked her shoulder bag on her suitcase, and pulled out her phone when she saw Parker walking down the wide aisle. She quickly typed a text to Valeria.

> KELLI: Sleigh bells! I think he's coming to my gate!

> He can't be going on this retreat, too.

> There's no way he doesn't have somewhere to go for Christmas.

> No way.

> Oh, no. He's sitting down. Please tell me he has family in South Carolina.

> We just happen to be going to the same state. That's all.

> VALERIA: No way there's that big of a coincidence. He's going to the retreat.

> Kelli! DATE HIM!

> Oh my goodness, that's perfect.

Kelli rolled her eyes.

> KELLI: We tried that once before, remember? It was a disaster. Most awkward date ever.

> VALERIA: Just because you accidentally wore two different boots on the date doesn't mean you can't try again.

Kelli cringed at the memory. When she had put on two different boots, she had planned to see which one looked better. But then Parker texted, saying that he was lost and thought he got the address wrong, and she'd forgotten that she hadn't swapped into the winning pair before he got there. As people kept staring at her the whole date, she assumed it was because her outfit was pretty incredible. Because minus the boot issue, it was.

KELLI: You forgot about me knocking his soda into his lap at the movie theater during that jump scare.

Or that I had to leave the movie early because I got food poisoning from dinner.

Or that our waiter just happened to be someone I had dated and made comments about it the entire meal.

Those kinds of things don't exactly lend themselves to second dates.

VALERIA: Yep. Any relationship between the two of you is doomed before it even starts.

No use even trying.

KELLI: Stop it. They're boarding us now, so sorry—no more time for sarcasm. Talk to you tonight!

Kelli pushed the phone into its pocket on her bag and then wheeled her suitcase over to where everyone was lining up. Once she got on the plane, she put her suitcase in the overhead bin and her bag under the seat in front of her. The seat on her plane ticket was the middle one, which was fine by her. That meant double the people to talk to during take-off, the part that made her the most nervous.

Plus, the middle seat was close enough to the window

that she could see out without having to ask two people to move if she needed to go to the restroom mid-flight.

She looked up just in time to see Parker sit down in the aisle seat of the row right in front of her. What she'd told Valeria was true—this was a bad time for her to get into a relationship. But still, a part of her heart had hoped for a little bit of Christmas romance in her life, even though she knew the pain it would bring.

Except not with Parker.

That obviously wouldn't work. That one date they'd gone on two-and-a-half years ago had been only a couple of months after she started working at ZentCube, and it had made work so awkward. She had constantly been reminded of the experience and embarrassed all over again. It was not something she was looking to repeat anytime soon.

Even if he did look mighty fine in his jeans and t-shirt—something she never saw him in at the office. Nope. She was completely ignoring him and not even noticing how good he looked at all.

Instead, she chatted with the nice young man to her left who was flying home for Christmas and was very excited about it, and the mom on her right who was flying with her kids to visit their grandparents. The woman was nervous because she hadn't seen her ex-in-laws in over three years and they always made her so uncomfortable. But she'd gotten a call last minute saying that her ex-father-in-law was sick and probably didn't have long to live, so they booked flights just the night before and couldn't even sit together.

The woman's story was fascinating, so before Kelli knew

it, the plane was at cruising altitude and she had barely even noticed anything else during takeoff. Both of her seatmates seemed to be done talking, so she pulled out her headphones, plugged them into her phone, and started listening to an audiobook.

Through the teeny space between the seats, she had the perfect view of Parker. So she just enjoyed the curve of the muscles on his arm and the perfect amount of scruff along that strong jawline.

He leaned forward to get his water bottle out of his bag, and she got to see his back muscles in action through his t-shirt. He flipped open the spout of the water bottle, and because of the change in pressure on the plane, a big burst of water shot through the straw and up in the air in a perfect arc, right in her direction.

She didn't have time to do anything—not that she could've done anything, since she was trapped in the middle seat and wearing a seatbelt—before the water landed right on her lap.

She let out a yelp of surprise, along with the handful of other people who witnessed it, as the cool liquid soaked through her pants.

Parker immediately turned around, an embarrassed, apologetic look on his face, before he noticed that it was her that his water had landed on. Then she swore his expression turned to one that said this was payback for her spilling his drink in his lap on their date so long ago.

He did press the button to call a flight attendant, though, and the nice lady got her plenty of paper towels to soak it up. But her efforts didn't exactly leave her jeans dry. *Please let them dry before we land,* she silently prayed. She could only imagine how embarrassing it would be to walk through the airport once they landed looking like she'd had an accident on the plane. Especially with Parker there to see it.

She didn't know the eleven others who were going on this same retreat (and she refused to believe that Parker was one of them), but she suspected she would know them well by the end of the week. She didn't want wet pants to be their first impression of her.

Once the excitement of the surprise fountain and the soaked lap died down, the cabin lights dimmed, and everyone with window seats around her started closing the shades. Between the lowered lights and the hum of the airplane, drowsiness hit her pretty strongly.

Her dad had come over to "spend Christmas" with her last night before they both left on their separate trips, and she couldn't bear to cut the evening short to pack when she got to see him so infrequently lately. Plus, she kind of wanted to remind him that she was his daughter and they had a bond. She had to do all she could to make sure she wasn't forgotten.

So he left late, and she stayed up even later packing. Then she had to wake up super early to get ready for the day, finish packing, drive to airport parking—which had been a bear of a drive with all the holiday traffic—take the shuttle to the airport, go through security, and still make it to her flight without being rushed. And she was feeling the lack of sleep now.

The audiobook could wait. She wrapped her headphone cord nice and neat, slipped it into its pocket in her bag, slid her phone in alongside it, then pulled out her neck pillow and drifted off to sleep.

Six

PARKER

PARKER PULLED his ear buds from his ears. He'd been watching a movie on the screen attached to the seat in front of him when the five-year-old seated next to him whom he'd been chatting with at the beginning of the flight started crying.

"Hey, buddy. Do you need help with anything?"

The kid shook his head, but he still kept crying. Not a loud cry—just an upset one.

"Are you hungry? I still have my cookies from when they brought us snacks."

Still, the boy just shook his head. Parker glanced at the teenage girl sitting by the window, and she just shrugged, like *Don't look at me—I don't know what to do.* He heard the flight attendant right behind him talking to someone. Maybe he could get her help afterward.

"Do you need something to drink? Or do you need to go to the bathroom?"

The boy shook his head. "I just want my mom."

The flight attendant tapped Parker on the shoulder, so he turned his attention to her. "Excuse me, sir. But do you mind switching seats with the boy's mother?"

"Oh, not at all. Of course." He hurried to pack his headphones, water bottle, and cookies into his shoulder bag, said goodbye to the kid, and then stood up to see where she wanted him to move to. The flight attendant was motioning to the aisle seat in the row directly behind him.

"Thank you so much," the boy's mom said before slipping into Parker's seat.

Parker nodded and then stared at the seat the woman had vacated. It was the one right next to Kelli. Maybe he should've asked where he'd be moving to before agreeing. At least Kelli was asleep—maybe they could avoid any awkward chatting. Especially if that chatting was going to end up being about his water landing in her lap. He sat down next to her and put his ear buds back in his ears.

He started the same movie again, hoping to pick up where he left off, but he was having trouble keeping his mind on it when he was so close to Kelli. Ever since he had caught the tail end of her phone conversation with James in the copy and print room years ago, he had forced himself to only think of her as a coworker. Even though James, from what he saw at a couple of company parties, wasn't nearly good enough for her.

And then he had started dating Stephanie. But now they were both single, and he was noticing her again in a way he hadn't allowed himself to for so long.

He didn't know why he was allowing himself to think about her now. As Stephanie had not-so-nicely pointed out, he had enough flaws of his own to prove that he wasn't good enough for Kelli, either. Besides—he had thought he and his ex were happy and hadn't seen their breakup coming. He didn't trust himself to know when things were going wrong anymore.

He turned the volume on the movie up even more and made himself concentrate on it.

Which worked pretty well for a good thirty minutes. Then Kelli turned slightly in her sleep, and she leaned to rest her head on his chest and shoulder. The scent of her freshly-washed hair was right there.

He should wake her up.

Except she looked so peaceful and so relaxed. Maybe she needed the sleep. Maybe he could just nudge her enough to stay in her seat without waking her up. He slowly moved his shoulder, nudging her toward the middle of her seat. It took a minute, but he got her there. He carefully started pulling himself back, testing to make sure that she wasn't going to fall over when he wasn't holding her up.

Eventually, he got to where his shoulder wasn't touching her anymore, and he started breathing again as he moved back to his normal position in his seat.

But within five minutes she shifted again, her head finding his shoulder. She had the neck pillow, so that wasn't what had pulled her toward him. Maybe she just needed to lean on something.

Once, back when he was in college, he was on a bus

headed home for Christmas, and he fell asleep. He'd woken to find that he'd been leaning against the shoulder of a woman who was the age of his grandma. He'd been embarrassed, sure, but also really grateful. It had been the best sleep he had gotten in a while. Sometimes you're really tired and you need the kindness of the person sitting next to you to be a support. He could do that for Kelli. He just needed to turn the volume of the movie up louder to keep his thoughts off her.

When the captain's voice came over the intercom asking everyone to prepare the cabin for landing, Kelli jerked awake with a scream. Still looking like she was in the fog of sleep, she realized that she'd been leaning against someone's shoulder and seemed embarrassed and unwilling to make eye contact. She wiped the edge of her mouth with her knuckles, which must have told her that she had been drooling because her eyes flew to his shoulder. Then she did make eye contact with him and jerked to more alertness.

"Parker! What are you doing here? Was I sleeping on you?" She reached out and wiped at the small wet spot she had left on his shirt, and then whacked at it with the back of her hand. "Why did you let me sleep on you?"

He couldn't help the smile. "Hey, don't blame me. I was just sitting here, minding my own business. You're the one who invaded my space. I tried to push you back."

Her cheeks were flushed, and against her blonde hair, which was straight and down—something he rarely saw when she was at work—it was beautiful.

"Well, maybe you should've tried harder."

"I should've. Your snoring was making it difficult for me to hear my movie."

Her eyes narrowed at him. "I did not snore." Then she turned to the guy on the other side of her. "Did I snore?"

He looked every bit as amused as Parker was, but shook his head no.

She faced forward in her seat, hands folded in her lap, a vindicated smile on her face, but he could see beneath the smile a residual embarrassment at having slept against his shoulder. Maybe he should've woken her up. Except if he had, she still would've realized that she'd fallen asleep on his shoulder and still would've been embarrassed—she just would've gotten an hour less sleep out of the deal.

The plane landed and taxied to the gate. When it was their turn to deplane, he stood up in the aisle and took a step back, motioning for Kelli to go first. An olive branch. She must've been feeling some embarrassment still, because she stood up, slung her bag over her shoulder, and then jerked her suitcase out of the overhead bin and started power walking up the aisle.

"Hey," the guy who had been sitting at the window said. Then he turned to Parker. "What's her name?"

"Kelli."

"Hey, Kelli! That's my bag!"

Kelli froze, her back to them, then she turned around, cheeks flushed even more, and walked back to their row as Parker pulled out the bag he was fairly certain was hers and set it on the floor in front of her. She strode with purpose out of the plane, head held high, shoulders back. Parker smiled at her the whole way.

They were heading in the same direction, so even though Kelli had gotten the head start, she eventually must've brushed off the embarrassment, because she stopped moving like she was trying to win a speed-walking competition and started walking at a normal pace. He thought it was safer to be near her then, and before he knew it, they were walking side-by-side. He told himself he was drawn to her simply because she was the only person he knew in the state. It was just human nature.

"So," she eventually said, partially glancing in his direction but not enough for their eyes to meet, "is this a layover for you, or is this your final destination?"

"Final destination."

She gave a tight nod. "Do you have family in South Carolina?"

The tone of her voice was hopeful, but he had no problem dashing that hope. "Nope. I'm here for the ZentCube retreat." It wasn't hard to guess that she was, too.

She turned her head away from him, but he didn't miss the grimace on her face before she did.

As they were riding down the escalators leading to baggage claim, she grabbed his arm with her free hand and said, "Look! They sent drivers to get us!" As soon as she realized she was holding onto his arm, though, she let go.

All Parker could think about was the way it felt to have Kelli's hand on his arm, and how empty it felt to have it disappear so quickly. But he did look in the direction she had pointed to see two drivers in black suits with black driving caps, and they were both holding signs that said ZentCube on them.

After getting their luggage, it became obvious who the twelve of them going on the retreat were as they all gathered around the two drivers. Parker recognized several people from company functions, and one from working on a project with some people in building B—he was pretty sure the guy's name was Davis—but didn't know anyone else well enough to know their names. The twelve of them split up, six to a car, which ended up being a limo. The kind with two bench seats that faced each other.

As they made the drive from the airport to the resort, Kelli kept looking from window to window, trying to take in all the sights. He didn't think he was the only one in the car who probably would've missed them if Kelli hadn't been so enthusiastic about seeing everything.

He liked it when people appreciated all the amazing things surrounding them. He always had. How had he forgotten that so fully when he'd been making wedding plans with a woman who was impressed by nothing? How had he lost that part of himself while they'd been dating and engaged? It was a good thing that Stephanie had called it off.

Huh. That was a new thought. He had been crushed when his ex had ended things, and he hadn't quite gotten over feeling bad about that. His realization that it was a good thing felt like a piece of his shattered heart was just put back in place.

But that didn't mean he should be thinking of Kelli. She

deserved someone better than him. She deserved someone whose list of faults wasn't a mile long.

Kelli turned around and knocked on the window between them and the driver. It slid down. "Yes?"

"Um, that sign said that the check-in for the Royal Palm Resort was right back there."

The woman driving said, "That's not where you're checking in."

Suddenly everyone in the car was more on alert, watching exactly where they were going, all with confused faces. Their driver made a left turn, then drove past the main buildings for the hotel, past cottages, and turned right onto a road that ran slightly uphill but alongside the ocean to where several mansions stood tall and proud, and pulled to a stop at one.

"We're staying in a mansion?" Kelli exclaimed.

Their driver got out and opened their door, and Parker and the others all climbed out. "You can head inside," she said. "I'll get your luggage taken care of."

The other limo had pulled up right behind them, and the twelve of them stared up at the mansion in awe as they made their way to the front door. When Graham and Merit first told Parker about the retreat, this wasn't exactly what he had pictured.

Graham opened the front door right as they reached it and said, "Welcome! Come on, come inside—we're excited to get this week started!"

Parker stepped into a tall foyer of a mansion that opened in one direction to a living room and the other to a twisting staircase leading to a second floor, with a towering Christmas tree nestled in the curve of the staircase, all of which looked like a Christmas explosion had gone off. This place was even more decorated for the season than his Grandma Ines's house always was.

It appeared that escaping all of Christmas was going to be more difficult than he had planned.

$\mathcal{S}$even

KELLI

WHEN GRAHAM WELCOMED Kelli and the others into
the mansion, he immediately led them to a gigantic room
that had a family room on one side, a dining room on the
other, and a kitchen in the middle, and Kelli was in love. The
dining table seated sixteen people. Sixteen! A lunch buffet
was set up along one side of the room, which was good
because Kelli was starving.

Once they had their plates filled with a variety of cute
little sandwiches and different kinds of salads, they all sat
down at the big table. With Graham, Merit, and a woman
who didn't come in with them but was looking at Merit like
she was in love, they nearly filled the entire table.

For a while, they just chatted while they ate, and it felt
like heaven, being surrounded by so many happy people.
Parker was sitting straight across from her, and he looked like
he was enjoying it, too. Then, as they got close to finishing,
Graham stood up, and everyone stopped talking.

"Welcome, everyone. We're thrilled you joined us this Christmas."

Someone in a Royal Palms Resort uniform appeared from some side room and started clearing away everyone's plates while he spoke.

"I understand how it feels to not have anywhere to go for Christmas. I spent two years living away from family, and the holidays were especially rough. I know how it can make you long for all the traditions of home. Or how it can make you not want anything to do with Christmas at all. I completely understand that some of you are going to want to gravitate toward activities at the resort that don't have to do with Christmas, and you plan to skip anything we do here that's Christmassy, too."

From the corner of her eye, she saw Parker exhale in relief like he was so glad that Graham understood. Did he not like Christmas?

Merit stood up. "Our goal," he said as he motioned between him and Graham, "is to make sure that you don't."

Kelli didn't want to be obvious by turning to look at Parker so she couldn't see his response to Merit's declaration, but she chuckled inside knowing that he probably wasn't thrilled about it.

"Okay, *make sure you don't* is kind of harsh. We're going to *encourage* you to participate. Because we know that when we get to the end of this week, you're going to be happier and more refreshed if you do."

"Now hop up," Graham said. "We have explaining to do, and explaining is always better with a slideshow!"

Everyone looked at each other, seeming just as wary of the slideshow as she was. Especially because this was supposed to be a break from work. But they still stood, of course, looking around to see where they should go.

"Don't look so afraid," Merit said. "Graham's presentations aren't boring."

Joy, a quiet, sweet, and adorable woman who had ridden in the same limo as Kelli, walked up to Kelli and said, "I don't know a soul here. Do you?"

"Just Parker." She motioned at him as they walked toward the couches on the family room side of the room.

"He is one good-looking guy."

"Yeah," she sighed. "If only he wasn't Parker."

"Oh. He's bad news, then?"

She shook her head. "Only for me."

The couches were a giant half-circle facing a fireplace with a huge TV above it. An undecorated Christmas tree stood next to the fireplace, looking regal and ready to be loved. Kelli sat on the couch with everybody else and, once again, realized she had sat with Parker in her line of sight.

"Welcome to the ZentCube Christmas Celebration!" Graham said, the first slide of his slideshow appearing on the screen. It was of each of their faces—pulled from their employee ID badges—on tiny bodies, looking like bobble-heads dancing. The sound of a crowd cheering played with it, and everyone laughed, including Kelli. She knew the cheering wasn't real, but still, it made it feel more festive and exciting.

"Now, we have a little contest to get you all in the

Christmas spirit. There are two parts to this—individual activities and group activities." Graham switched to a new slide, and a little bobble-headed Merit danced onto the top of the screen, with a list of activities below him. "Now, during your time here, you can do any of these activities, and each one will earn you one point. All you have to do is send a picture of you doing the activity to Merit and me."

Two phone numbers came up on the screen, and Graham paused while they all pulled out their phones and entered them in. Kelli couldn't believe that Merit and Graham were giving them their personal cell phone numbers. She was putting the CEO's and the CTO's phone numbers into her phone!

"Feel free to take a picture of this slide if you'd like, but just know that all of these activities, along with where to go to do them, are posted on that wall over there. Now, Merit is going to talk about the group activities."

Graham changed the slide as Merit stood, and this time, all twelve of their bobble-heads danced their way to the top of the screen, to the sounds of people shouting things like "Yay! My favorite!" and "I can't wait!" along with a lot of clapping.

"I would like to introduce you all to Elise Stevens." Merit motioned to the woman who had been sitting next to him, with a look of utter adoration on his face. Like she was his world, and everything shone brighter with her in it. And Elise looked back at Merit like she had discovered the secret to happiness when she had met him.

The woman was probably a couple of years younger than Kelli, yet she had already found a love like that. Someday, Kelli was going to find a man who would look at her that way when he introduced her to people. And she was going to look at him the same way Elise was looking at Merit.

"Elise is the activities director for the Royal Palm Resort, and the reason why this resort is so popular at Christmastime."

Elise blushed, which made Kelli smile. And then, for some stupid-crazy reason, Kelli found her eyes darting to Parker. She had to remind herself that she was in no position to date right now. And especially not if that date was Parker. The two of them had already tested those waters, so they already knew they'd sink. She didn't want to date *anyone* in her building again, actually. It made for too much awkwardness.

"Be down here for breakfast every morning at nine," Merit continued. "For those of you counting, yes, that's seven Denver time. Don't worry—we'll make the meal worth your while. And that's when Elise will talk about the itinerary for the day, including the group activities. You'll want to join in on them because they'll be worth two points each. Graham, want to tell them what their points will buy?"

Graham stood again, a grin spread across his face. "Do you remember that work satisfaction survey that went out to random employees via email a week or so ago? Yeah, that only went out to the twelve of you. And the question we were most looking for your answers to was the one that read, 'What kind of non-monetary reward would most motivate you?'

"So we took your answers and came up with a prize package. We're hoping there's at least one thing on this list that will make each of you want to earn as many points as possible so that you can win it."

Graham changed to a new slide, and a little game show host walked onto the screen, motioning big with her arms at one of three wrapped presents. "The first prize we are offering is," he dragged out the word, then the present burst open, "three bonus vacation days, to be used whenever you'd like over the next year."

There were lots of "Ooh!"s and "Wow!"s from the group, but that prize didn't really interest Kelli. She glanced at Parker and saw that he didn't seem particularly interested, either.

"And the next prize is..." The game show host moved and then motioned big at the second of the three prizes on the screen. It burst open and Graham said, "A free catered lunch for everyone on your team, delivered once a week every week for a full year!"

Kelli's eyes went wide. She instantly wanted this prize, and she wanted it badly. She imagined how much everyone on her team would enjoy it. How much all their faces would light up each week when it came. How valuable it would make her to the team, and how much she would enjoy being the one who won it for them. How much of a great bonding thing it would be for everyone on her team. With that kind of experience every week, her team would be unstoppable.

She could feel Parker's eyes on her, so she glanced over at him and saw a look of curious interest—but only until she looked. He quickly dropped the expression and turned his attention to the TV again.

"And for the last prize." The little character Vanna White-ed the last gift, and it burst open. "The best parking spot at your building for a full year! We polled a bunch of people at each building to find out which was the most coveted spot." Then he read the list of buildings and the parking spot they were giving away at each one. "And for building C—so marketing, sales, and accounting—spot C-seven."

Kelli gasped and her eyes immediately found Parker's, and they stared at each other. Kelli hadn't looked at him when Graham mentioned the second prize, but based on the expression on his face right now, even if he hadn't been interested in the lunch, he was definitely interested in the parking space.

The competition was on, and Kelli intended to win it.

"It looks like we've got you interested," Merit said, chuckling. "You'll see that right next to the list of individual activities on that wall, there's a bar chart with each of your names, and we'll update it with the number of points you currently have as soon as you report them. And just to the right of that, we'll have the daily group activity posted."

"And this won't stop on Christmas Day," Graham added. "We aren't a fan of the let-down you feel when all celebration stops the moment Christmas is over. We'll be celebrating up until the morning of the twenty-eighth, which is when the retreat ends.

"At that point, you are welcome to fly back home or you can stay here until New Year's Day. We won't be doing the retreat for the extra days, so you'll be on your own for most things, but we'll still have the mansion. So you can keep your room and take advantage of all The Royal Palm has to offer. Just let us know in the next few days which day you'd like to fly home."

Kelli's eyebrows rose. She hadn't expected at all that they might offer more days. Her dad was going to be returning from his trip on the 29th, and she kind of wanted to be home when he arrived.

Merit nodded. "I'll be here until New Year's Day, but Graham is going to head home on Monday for a family Christmas party. He'll be back in time for our Christmas Eve celebrations, and when he comes back, he'll have his wife, Tessa, and his little baby, Hope, with him."

"Who just happens to be the cutest baby in the universe!" Graham added, which made Kelli smile.

Graham switched to a new slide, one with Santa sneaking into a room. "We are doing Secret Santas, too, and Merit's assistant, Carla, randomly chose a name for each of you. When you get to your room, you'll find an envelope on your nightstand with the name of the person you'll be a Secret Santa for. Throughout your time here, try to get to know that person, and then get a small gift for them to open on Christmas morning."

"Your luggage is already in your rooms," Merit said, "which are on the two floors above us, and your room assignments are posted on the same wall over there with the points. The theater and the exercise room are downstairs. But before we let you go up and get settled, we have our first group activity!"

Elise, the woman Merit had introduced as the resort's activities director, stood for the first time. "We have a tree that needs decorating, but there are no decorations because you all are going to be the ones to make them."

All twelve of them looked at each other as if any of them understood what the plan was.

"We've got some supplies set up on the table back there," Elise said.

Kelli turned to look—someone had apparently come in while they were watching the presentation and set everything up. She hadn't even heard it happening.

Elise shook a box. "And I've got a bunch of different themes right here. Everyone partner up. Each partnership needs to come grab a theme, then make at least four ornaments with that theme."

Without letting her brain have a second to think about it or to give her eyes permission, Kelli's attention flew to Parker. Apparently, he'd done the same, because they were suddenly looking at each other. It would've been awkward to just turn away, so she raised an eyebrow in a silent question, asking if he wanted to be her partner for the activity. Parker only hesitated a second before a strange look crossed his face and he turned to the woman next to him—

someone Kelli hadn't met yet—and asked her to be his partner.

Stupid eyes, thinking they could go and do the asking on their own. Her brain knew not to ask Parker—she didn't know why her eyes couldn't get the message. She exhaled, and then she stood up as everyone else did and looked around the group.

A man stepped over to her and said, "Hi. I'm Davis. Would you like to be my partner for this?"

He was cute. Nothing like Parker, of course, but he had a kind face and welcoming eyes, and looked like he might be in his late twenties, so that was perfect. His dark hair was the right amount of tussled, too. And he looked a little bit nervous to ask, which was pretty adorable. Not that she was looking to date anyone, but she wasn't against a little harmless flirting. Especially with someone who worked in a different building.

"I'm Kelli, and I would love to."

They grabbed their theme from the box Elise held—a paper that read *Santa's Workshop*—and headed over to the tables to get to work.

As they were looking at what kinds of supplies they had to work with and started brainstorming what they could make, Kelli's eyes couldn't help but find Parker again. He and the woman he teamed up with seemed to be having fun. They were picking up craft supplies and talking and laughing. She told herself that it was a good thing. Parker and his fiancée had called things off just a couple of months ago, so he probably really needed a chance to chat with a woman in a low-pressure situation.

Kelli wasn't jealous.

She wasn't wishing it was her with Parker instead of this other woman.

Nope. She was perfectly happy doing this activity with Davis. Her mind wasn't on Parker at all. Not one bit.

Eight

PARKER

BY THE LOOK on Kelli's face, she'd known that Parker understood that she wanted to be partners. And she knew that he'd pretended not to notice and instead turned to the person next to him. But he also knew that she hadn't meant to look his direction—she had just turned to him because they were the only ones from their building who were there, so he was likely the only person she knew. It was human nature. It wasn't because she wanted to be his partner.

Besides, she seemed super interested in all the Christmas activities, and he wasn't. At all. So he didn't want the simple human nature of seeking out the familiar being the thing that stopped her from enjoying the festivities.

Kelli had chatted with so many people since they had gathered together in a group at baggage claim that he figured she could easily partner with one of them. But couldn't it have been anyone other than Davis who asked her? Parker often worked with product development in Building B, since they needed to show off the latest in trade shows. He didn't work with Davis directly and didn't know him well, but he had been in the building enough to know that he was a pretty decent guy. He wasn't sure why that bothered him. He should be happy for Kelli.

Besides, he was kind of enjoying turning a bunch of random craft stuff into "Christmas on the Range" ornaments with Addison. She was funny, and they came up with some pretty brilliant ideas. And since it wasn't something he did as a tradition with his own family, it didn't make him feel sad about not being around them.

But he kept finding his eyes going to Kelli and Davis every time they laughed or every time they were working on something intricate and both were leaned in close together.

Which was ridiculous, especially since he wasn't in a position to date anyone—most of all Kelli. And if he had no interest in dating Kelli, he had no business caring how close she and Davis were right now. Or that he just brushed a lock of hair over her shoulder for her so it wouldn't get in the glue she was using.

"So, which of the three prizes do you most want to win?"

Addison's question had caught him off guard enough that he told himself that he needed to focus more on what he was doing instead of on what Kelli was doing. "Oh, um, parking spot, hands down."

"Really? The parking space?" Addison scrunched up her nose in confusion.

"It's a great parking spot."

"Is it hard to get a good one at your building?"

"Not really. I usually get there at seven, so I mostly have my pick. Except for that one—it always gets taken first."

"But your second place choice can't be more than five steps further from the door at seven."

The second place choice was closer to the door. That wasn't what it was about. And suddenly he wondered what it was actually about. How much did he love the space because of the space, and how much did he love it because of the competition to get it between him and Kelli?

He didn't know why, but simply the thought of it made him suddenly need to compete for that parking space while they were here. Maybe if he just stayed away from the things his own family normally did at Christmastime, it wouldn't be so hard.

"How about you?"

"Time off," Addison said. "I love traveling to new places, and an extra three days would make that even better."

"What have been your favorite places to travel to?"

Addison started telling him, and he tried hard to listen, but he kept noticing how organized Kelli was with the craft supplies she was working with. There were twelve people around the table working, and it looked like an explosion of scissors, glues, paints, brushes, and all the craft supplies they'd been given to make the ornaments with.

Except for right in front of him and right in front of Kelli. Everything was lined up so neatly and orderly that she could find anything she needed quickly.

"How about you? Do you have any favorite places you've traveled?"

Okay, he had to be more serious about not letting his eyes or his mind wander to the other side of the table. So he talked with Addison as they finished making their four ornaments.

When Elise called time, Parker and Addison looked at their ornaments. He admired the horse they'd made out of brown felt that stood next to a cactus that was decorated like a Christmas tree, and the cowboy hat with mistletoe on the brim. He was pretty proud of what they had created once he'd quit looking in Kelli's direction. Elise had them all gather up their ornaments and bring them to the tree, and then Graham said, "Let the Christmas tree decorating begin!"

Addison hung two of them, and Parker searched for the perfect spot for their other two, as all twelve of them were gathered around the same tree, trying to find places for theirs.

Before he knew it, he was reaching to put one of his up high while someone was reaching in front of him to place one, and he looked down to see that Kelli was pressed against him, their faces less than a foot apart. There was so much jostling around the tree that someone knocked into Kelli, and he had barely placed his ornament in time to put his arm on her shoulders to keep her from falling.

Her eyes held his for a small moment as they stood inches apart, sharing the same air, electricity seeming to crackle between them, before she cleared her throat and said,

"Thank you," and then looked away. He quickly turned away from her gaze, too, and his eyes landed on her ornament.

"Wow, Kelli." He leaned in closer to it. There were little elves with wooden marble faces and felt bodies, wearing tall pointed hats with a mini pompom on top. They were both kneeling on the floor, wrapping gifts. Differently colored wrapping paper covered the floor, and she had even taken curling ribbon, cut in half so it was thinner, and made little tiny bows out of it. The amount of detail in such a small space was mind-blowing. "This is incredible. So intricate. I'm impressed."

He looked back at her to see that she was beaming at the compliment. She should be.

Once all the ornaments were placed and they had all stepped back, Graham turned the tree lights on and led them all in the *ooh*ing and *aah*ing. It did look decent. Nothing like home, though, which caused a wave of melancholy to wash over him. But then he glanced at Kelli and saw the joy on her face as she stared at the tree in wonder. It made him look back at it again. For not being like the one at home, it was a good tree.

Graham clapped his hands together. "Okay, you've got two hours to head to your room and get settled. Your packing list asked you to bring the most formal outfit you had. When you come back, be wearing that, because we're headed to the Tinsel and Tidings Christmas feast and ball!"

Parker headed to his room, which was so much more impressive than his room in his apartment. His suitcases were waiting for him, just like Merit said they'd be, so he started unpacking them and hanging up his clothes. Then he saw the envelope on his nightstand and remembered about the Secret Santa. He set down the shirt he'd been about to hang up and walked over to it. He opened the envelope, looked at the name printed inside, and smiled.

Kelli Ellis

Once he got all of the items put in a closet, drawer, or in the bathroom, he still had about an hour and fifty minutes before they had to be dressed and downstairs.

He looked around the giant room and exhaled. Getting ready would only take about thirty minutes. Being in this room just made him realize even more strongly how alone he was, and he couldn't spend the extra hour and twenty minutes here or he was going to go crazy.

He headed down to the second floor, but there wasn't a soul in the family room or kitchen, so he headed to the basement to check it out. The exercise room had several machines and a good number of free weights. He'd have to take advantage of them while he was here.

The theater was impressive, too. It seated twenty-one people in three rows, all in reclining chairs. And in between the theater and exercise room were several table games. He walked over to the ping pong table, grabbed a paddle and ball, and started bouncing it on the paddle over and over.

Down here was just as depressing as his room. Maybe he just needed to leave the mansion and explore a bit. He set the paddle and the ball down and had taken one step toward the door when Kelli walked into the room. "Oh, hi. You're not spending the extra time resting from travel, huh?"

Kelli laughed. How had he not noticed how amazing of a laugh she had before now? "I got my rest from travel on the plane, remember?"

He chuckled and smiled again at the memory of her being so close as she lay her head on his shoulder. "You up for a game?"

"We *could*," Kelli said. "Or we could get a jump start on everyone else and do something that will earn us some points."

Parker looked at the pool table. The game sounded like a lot more fun—he really wasn't in the mood to do anything else that was Christmassy after making the tree decorations. "What do you have in mind?" He wanted to know exactly what they'd be doing before he would be willing to commit.

Kelli pulled out her phone, probably to see the picture she had taken during the presentation. "Oh! One of them is to walk along the beach and write a Christmas message or draw a Christmas scene with a stick in the sand. That would be fun, and I have been dying to check out the beach."

A walk on the beach wasn't Christmassy, and he didn't have to draw a picture if he didn't want to. He could do that.

Less than five minutes later, they were both walking along the beach. It had only been a short pathway from the mansion, and the weather was nice. Easily over fifty degrees and sunshiny, so it felt warm enough without wearing jackets.

The beach was nearly empty, which surprised him. Sure, it was too cold to play in the sand and water, but it was still beautiful out. Kelli had changed into flip-flops, and she took them off and ran along the sand at the edge of the water, scrambling out of the way whenever a wave came in, and squealing when it washed over her feet because she didn't make it far enough onto the beach in time.

He smiled as he watched her.

"Take off your shoes! It's not that cold. Still tons warmer than anywhere in Colorado right now."

That was true. Why not? Anything to take his mind off Christmas. He left his shoes and socks on a bench and went out to the water's edge. The sand was soft beneath his feet and felt great. He hadn't been to a beach in far too long.

Before he knew it, he wasn't only dodging the waves coming in—he was also dodging Kelli's kicks of water she was sending in his direction. He sent plenty back in her direction. And as she said, it wasn't too cold, especially since he had already acclimated to the Colorado winter.

At least, it wasn't too cold until he didn't dodge Kelli's splash of water. He gasped as the cold water soaked his pants. "Is this to get even for my water bottle on the plane? Because that wasn't my fault."

"And it wasn't my fault that you didn't move fast

enough to get out of the way of that last one." There was a teasing glint in her eyes and a grin on her face as she sent another splash of water his way that he *did* move away from fast enough, and then she took off running to get away from any retaliation.

So, of course, he ran after her. He would run after her as long as it took to catch her.

"Whoa," he said out loud as he slowed to a walk. Where had that thought come from? He was not chasing Kelli. He wasn't trying to date her. He wasn't looking for a relationship at all. He hadn't guessed that coming out here, seeing her running free and happy along the beach would be a bad idea. A dangerous idea.

The walk got his mind off Christmas and how he thought he'd be spending it. Now he just needed something to take his mind off Kelli.

Kelli had stopped running, too, but she had stopped because she had found a few sticks that had washed ashore. He could've left right then and gone back to the mansion. But just because he was having a crisis of motivation didn't mean he was just going to leave her out there alone.

Plus, he wanted points for this activity, too. He couldn't let her get ahead already.

That was all. He was here for the points.

Kelli drew a gigantic, very fancy "Merry Christmas" in the sand. Parker wasn't going to draw anything Christmas-related, but then a memory of one of his favorite Christmases came to mind. His brother Ethan had somehow talked their parents into letting them sleep in sleeping bags in front of the tree so they could see Santa when he came to bring them presents, so he decided to draw that.

When he was finishing up, Kelli came over to look at it. "Wow. You're quite the artist."

"Isn't everyone who is drawn to marketing as a career?"

She shrugged. "To some degree, I guess. Not often this much. Is this you and your brother?"

Parker nodded as he finished drawing the scene in the sand. "We had fun. It was when Ethan was three and I was fifteen. I'd stopped believing in Santa before he was even born, but having a little brother who was that much younger than me let me relive the magic of Christmas all over again. I mean, you should've seen the excitement on Ethan's face when we woke up and saw that Santa had come while we were asleep."

When he finally looked up at Kelli, she had a curious expression on her face. The afternoon sun was right behind her, making her look like an angel as she gazed at his scene, and it made him wish all over again that he was good enough for her. "It sounds like you love Christmas."

He set down the stick and brushed off his hands, then stood up, brushing sand from his knees. "Usually. I've always wondered which had made me like Christmas more —my parents' love of the holiday, or getting a second chance at experiencing the magic of Christmas through a brother who was so much younger than me." He hoped that one day soon he'd be able to experience that all over again with his own kid. "But this year's different. I'm not a fan of Christmas this year, and I would happily skip it all."

"Is your family not around this year?"

He shook his head. "My parents went on a cruise to celebrate their thirtieth anniversary. They didn't think they'd be leaving me alone because I was supposed to be on a cruise myself right now."

He didn't know why he'd felt the need to get that off his chest. Maybe he just needed someone to know. Maybe he needed Kelli, specifically, to know. He knew the second that she had figured it all out because her hands flew to her mouth and she gasped. "Oh my gosh, it was supposed to be a honeymoon cruise, wasn't it?"

He nodded.

"I am so sorry."

He shrugged. "It was for the best. I hadn't believed it was at the time and didn't think I ever would, but now I get it that it was."

They both looked down at the pictures they had carved in the sand, but he wasn't sure either of them was actually seeing their drawings.

"I know what you mean."

Parker's eyes flew to Kelli, hoping she would say more.

"James and I broke up too, you know. He was the one to break it off, and it had crushed me. I didn't think I would ever feel like it was a good thing. But it's been a year, and I realized months ago that I had been in love with his family, not him. It was a big, beautiful family with so many different personalities, and I felt like I fit right in with them. Like they were my family.

"It wasn't until several months later that I finally understood that my relationship with James hadn't exactly been stellar. I had been letting the love I felt for his family color everything, so I hadn't even noticed that things weren't okay between us."

He knew exactly how it felt to not notice. He shook his head and chuckled. "Well, then, it looks like we both have our exes to thank for figuring things out for us."

She laughed, too. "I'll be sure to send him a thank you card." She looked at the things they had drawn in the sand. "Want to take pictures?"

Parker used Kelli's phone to take a picture of her standing just above her Christmas greeting, in a mid-air leap, arms thrown into the sky. Then he stood next to his, doing his best impression of the animated character in Graham's slide show that announced the prizes, and Kelli took a picture with his phone.

He was happy with the scene he had created. Even if it did make him miss Christmas at home.

As they headed back along the beach toward the mansion and the shoes they had both left behind, they texted their pictures to Graham and Merit as proof that they had completed the challenge.

"I can't believe we are texting the owners of ZentCube like they're our BFFs. I never thought I'd be doing this."

Parker looked over at Kelli as they walked along a beach, fifteen hundred miles from home, with the sun low in the sky, casting her in golden light. "I never thought I would, either."

Nine

KELLI

KELLI LOVED DRESSING FANCY. She had packed three elegant dresses when she saw it on the packing list, but she knew the one she was going to go for all along. It was the perfect shade of Christmas red, it was shimmery, and she always felt on fire when she wore it. Like she could do anything. She paired it with some equally fabulous red shoes.

Then she pulled her curled hair up in a loose bun that was speedy to do but looked all fancy, which made the dangly silver earrings she wore stand out even more.

Valeria texted to ask how things were going, so she texted back a picture of her in her dress, taken in the full-length mirror in the room.

VALERIA: Wow! You are going to knock the socks off all the guys there!

I mean MY socks just jumped off my feet.

Kelli smiled and texted the emoji with a girl dancing in a red dress. And then added lasers to it before sending it, laughing to herself.

> VALERIA: I see you chose the red dress. Does that mean you met an interesting, single guy?

Parker came to mind first, which shouldn't have surprised her, since she'd just spent an hour on the beach with him. But she reminded herself that a relationship with *anyone* wasn't a good idea right now, and a casual one with Parker would only make working on the same floor with him even more awkward than it had been after the last time they had dated. *Davis. Think only of Davis.*

> KELLI: I did, actually!

> His name is Davis, and he works in Development.

And, because she knew Valeria would ask for details, she added a text that said, *AND HE HAS NICE EYES*.

Valeria responded with the surprised emoji. Then the gasping emoji. Then the heart-eyes emoji.

> VALERIA: Wow. This is huge. Dipping a toe in the dating pool after so long. I'm so proud.

> Okay, I'll stop distracting you. You just go get your flirt on, girl!

> But don't you dare forget to text me the details later.

> KELLI: I won't.

She slipped her phone into her handbag, took one last look in the mirror, and then headed out her door. She was sure she wasn't heading down late at all, but as she walked down the curved staircase, she saw all six of the men already standing in the lobby, waiting. And she didn't miss their appreciative expressions. It was a little confirmation that she hit the mark with her outfit.

Her eyes were on Davis as she walked down the stairs. He looked nice dressed up so fancy. His suit was well fitted, his hair looked good, and those kind eyes were like an accessory that made the outfit.

But as much as she tried to keep her eyes only on Davis, they went to Parker anyway, and she forgot how to breathe. His dark suit looked on him like suits had been designed for the express purpose of making Parker Brockbank irresistible. It was a deep, warm gray that brought out colors in his eyes that she hadn't seen before. Those eyes looked captivating. Intoxicating. Like they were reaching out to capture her.

His hair, which had looked beautifully windblown on the beach, now looked tame enough to be respectable, while still having a hint of wildness. His scruff was trimmed short and neat and she wanted to run her hands along that strong jawline of his. If Davis was a ten out of ten, Parker was an easy nine hundred and fifty-seven.

She was in so much trouble. She needed blinders

tonight, like the kind they put on horses. Then she could just keep her eyes on Davis and not see Parker at all. Davis was attractive. He seemed like a good guy, and from what she knew of Graham and Merit, they wouldn't have invited him if he wasn't.

Davis, she told herself. Then, a little more firmly, she repeated *Davis. Keep your eyes on Davis.*

When she reached the bottom of the stairs, she stood on the side of Davis opposite Parker. Elise had talked with them earlier about this dinner and dance, and how she and her team had worked hard to make it a night that the people at the resort would enjoy. They all knew to head over to the ballroom, so as soon as the last person came down the stairs, the twelve of them went outside to find four golf carts in a row, waiting for them.

She and Davis weren't dating, though, and she didn't want him to get the impression that this was a date. Joy was walking next to her, so she linked arms with her new friend and they chatted as they walked to one of the carts, and both sat in the back seat. Another guy, Thomas, who she had seen Joy flirting with earlier, came and sat in the front seat next to the driver. Perfect.

Kelli hadn't seen much of the resort yet, but it was magical at night. Golden Christmas lights had been strung all over the grounds, across buildings, wound up palm trees, and lighting the pathways. This place was heaven.

And she was so grateful for the golf carts. It wouldn't have been a bad walk in regular shoes, but in four-inch heels when you wanted to dance the night away, not so much.

Their line of golf carts pulled up to a building, and before she knew it, Davis was at her side, offering her a hand out of the cart. She gave him a nod of thanks, took his hand, and stepped out of the cart. She didn't keep hold of his hand, though. She might be willing to dip a toe in the dating pool, but that was about it.

The ballroom was massive and had round tables in a half circle around the outside of the room. In one corner, three of the tallest Christmas trees she had ever seen were next to each other, each decorated with a different color scheme. One in silvers and blues, one in reds and greens, and one in golds. Garlands ran all along the room, all of which were decorated, and each table's centerpiece was practically a work of art.

When she imagined tonight as she was getting ready, she had been thinking about who she wanted to sit by and how she could maneuver things so that she wouldn't be near Parker. She knew that getting close to him was dangerous, and she had felt herself slipping when they'd been on the beach. Especially when he had been looking at the scene he had drawn in the sand that showed him with his little brother. But now? With him in that suit? Now would be particularly dangerous to be around him.

Figuring out how to get everyone to sit where she had imagined had been futile, though, because the hostess directed them to two tables, and each one had their name at a specific place. She found hers and sat down, and Davis sat to her right. And then, a moment later, Parker sat at her left.

It was fine.

She could pretend she had blinders.

Blinders, and amazing food. They hadn't been seated for long before the waiter brought in cinnamon-spiced sweet potato soup with maple croutons, which not only was an explosion of tasty goodness in her mouth but made her whole body rejoice at whatever was in it. She chatted with everyone at the table, and if she ever caught her mind wandering to Parker, she just took another bite.

And then the waiter brought in the main course—roasted pork loin with herb stuffing; Italian roasted cremini mushrooms, cauliflower, and tomatoes; and the softest, fluffiest rosemary dinner rolls that Kelli had ever tasted. The entire meal was so full of flavor and texture that she couldn't have asked for a better distraction. She cut each item into the perfect bite-sized pieces.

She speared a grape tomato and cut it in half, then attempted to spear one of the mushrooms to do the same. But somehow the fork slipped and, in a move she couldn't duplicate if she was paid to, she managed to send it airborne instead, and it landed with a plop in Parker's water goblet.

Several people at the table saw and let out an audible gasp and then restrained chuckles. The people who hadn't seen, Davis included, turned to see what had caused every-one's reaction.

Parker just lifted his glass and considered it. "I've had restaurants put lemons, limes, oranges, cucumbers, and even strawberries in my water before. This is the first time I've had a mushroom." And then he took a drink.

With as hot as her face and ears felt, she knew her cheeks were as red as her dress.

"I didn't get a mushroom in mine," Davis said, clearly not understanding what had just happened.

"I bet if you asked Kelli nicely, she could help you out with that."

Kelli closed her eyes, trying to make the embarrassment go away. She did everything right and planned precisely so that embarrassing things didn't happen. Yet they always seemed to happen around Parker no matter how hard she tried.

She speared a perfectly-cut piece of the stuffed pork and made herself focus on the bite by trying to pick out what spices were used. Was that cardamom? And maybe Juniper? She would keep trying to figure it out for as long as it took for her face to get back to a normal temperature.

When the waiter removed their dinner plates, she exhaled in relief because maybe she could get to the dancing and away from Parker. But then the waiter set dessert in front of each of them—a plate of vanilla bean clafoutis with raspberries and nectarines. It tasted amazing, but she only had three bites before she declared herself full and set down her fork.

A man's voice came over the sound system, and Kelli's attention turned to the man at the microphone who introduced himself as Christian, the dance instructor at the resort.

"We have a little custom here for the Tinsel and Tidings Ball. We like to start the first dance with our guests who have come in this week for dance lessons. They'll be showcasing the Viennese Waltz, and once they're done, we'd like to welcome you all to join us on the floor for an evening of dancing!"

As they watched the guests waltz, Davis leaned in her direction and said in a quiet voice, "Pretty impressive for only a week of dance lessons, don't you think?"

Kelli nodded. She had taken years of dance lessons, but never any ballroom. She could hold her own at a dance, but she always wished she knew how to ballroom dance.

The moment the song was over, Davis turned toward her, palm held upright, and said, "Would you like to dance?" like it was a race and he had to rush out of the gate.

"I would love to." She took his hand, stood, and let him lead her to the dance floor. She didn't even turn enough to glimpse Parker's face. She was staying so strong she should get an award. Plus, Davis hadn't witnessed all the embarrassing things she'd done—not just tonight but on this whole trip—so it felt nice to head to the dance floor with him.

As they danced, it was clear that Davis was getting his flirt on, too. It made her feel pretty. They weren't doing the Viennese Waltz, exactly, but dancing with Davis was easy. Nice.

More and more couples came onto the dance floor, and as they turned and moved around the floor, she saw some she recognized. Joy and Thomas were dancing, and it made Kelli smile. The two looked adorable together, and she hoped they might decide to start dating before the trip was over. They saw Merit and Elise, too, and Kelli once again felt that pang of longing for a relationship like theirs. They just looked so happy and radiant.

And then she saw Parker dancing with Addison, and she didn't care if she was supposed to let Davis lead—she turned them so that she wouldn't be seeing him. She didn't know why it was bothering her. It shouldn't. She and Parker knew they wouldn't work out. And even if she was wrong and things had changed over the past two-and-a-half years— which was a possibility—she knew *she* wouldn't work out with anyone right now. She was too vulnerable and needed to be cautious.

So she put on her blinders and focused on Davis, and he rewarded her with a big smile. They danced together for the next dance, too, and it was also nice. Then they headed back toward their table to grab some water.

As they neared, her eyes found Parker, like her attention was magnetically pulled toward him whether she liked it or not. He was chatting and laughing with a few people. A couple people were standing just outside the circle they made, looking at Parker's group like they wanted to join in but were shy or unsure. Parker spotted them, and so subtly shifted in a way that opened his circle. He said something to one of them, and just like that, the two others were in their group, chatting and laughing, too.

Why did he have to go and do sweet things like that? Couldn't he just shout at someone for stepping on his foot, punch someone in the gut, or bump into someone, knocking them down, and not apologize so she could get over him already?

Getting drinks of water put them right next to Parker's group and they quickly found themselves pulled into the group, and laughing and chatting themselves.

As they talked, she felt Davis's fingers brush up against hers. A question, a nudge, asking if he could hold her hand. She had imagined this being a night of fun, dancing with a lot of different people. Doing a little flirting, but nothing serious. Davis silently asking to hold her hand felt an awful lot like he was trying to claim her for the night. She liked dancing with him, but she didn't want that. So she just brought her hands together in front. A subtle move, but one that should get the point across to Davis.

A new song started, but she wasn't quite ready to leave the conversation yet, so she didn't so much as glance in the direction of the dance floor. Parker asked her, specifically, to say what her favorite cheese was when everyone was saying theirs, and right after she answered, Davis wrapped his arm around her back, placed his hand on her shoulder, and leaned in to whisper, "Did I mention how great you smell?"

And then he left his hand there. He had done it like he was pulling her close to tell her something, but it was as blatant as a guy stretching at a movie theater before draping his arm on a girl's shoulder. She didn't want to embarrass the guy by pushing his hand off her shoulder. He was a nice guy and was probably only doing it because he was feeling threatened by Parker. Who wouldn't? Parker looked like a movie star tonight.

So she waited a moment, then leaned forward to look at Joy's bracelet and shook his hand off her shoulder at the same time.

Except instead of taking the hint and dropping his arm to his side, he dropped it to her waist. She took in a slow, deep breath. If Davis was a jerk, there were several things she could do to make sure he got the message. But he wasn't, and she didn't want him to think that she wasn't interested in him at all or that she was mad at him. She simply didn't want someone to claim her as their date tonight.

As everyone in the circle chatted, she ran through options in her head of what could send the message but hadn't come up with any good ones when her eyes fell on Parker. He was studying her, reading the situation. He met her eyes, and it felt like a question. Like he was looking for confirmation that he was reading the situation correctly. She could've given him a slight nod but hadn't, yet somehow he still saw it in her eyes.

As soon as Joy finished what she was saying, Parker stepped into the circle toward Kelli. He held out a hand. "Would you like to dance?"

She smiled and put her hand in his. "I would."

She was sure that Davis got the message as she and Parker walked onto the dance floor, and she was so grateful.

The song ended seconds after they got to a spot on the dance floor, which was great because then she knew she'd get at least a full song with Parker. He kept one of her hands in his and placed his other hand in the middle of her back. Interesting. He didn't go for the waist. Not that she would have any problem with his hand on her waist, but between that and the amount of space between them, it felt like he was silently showing that he respected her.

She put her hand on his shoulder, resting her arm on his, which made her take in Parker in his suit with touch in addition to sight, and the extra sense nearly overwhelmed her.

"You are impressively graceful," Kelli said.

"I was going to say the same about you, but I was also going to add that you are extraordinarily beautiful."

"Wow. A good dancer and a good complimenter. Your mom must be so proud."

"She is. But to be fair, if Graham and Merit had us make macaroni art and I texted her a picture of it, she would be proud of me for that, too."

Kelli smiled. "She sounds like a great person."

"She really is."

Dancing with Davis had felt nice. Dancing with Parker felt amazing. Maybe it wouldn't be so bad to have someone claim her as their date tonight.

Wow, did that thought feel dangerous. It would definitely be bad to fall for him because she would still see him daily when this was over.

As the song was nearing the end, Parker pulled her closer and said in a voice that couldn't have been heard by anyone but her, "I got the impression that you don't want to be tied to one person tonight, right?"

She tried to nod, but now that she had Parker's arm around her, she wasn't so sure. She was currently having trouble simply remembering to breathe. He must've seen past that, though, because he said, "If you'd like to make sure that message gets across fully, Roman from QA is a good guy, and with as often as his eyes have gone to you, I'm sure he'd love to dance. If you'd like, I can lead us over there so it'd be natural for you to walk in his direction after the dance."

"Thanks," she managed to breathe as she marveled at this man.

She might have still been marveling at him when he thanked her for the dance and walked away just as they neared Roman from QA. Parker looked back at her once, but she hadn't been able to see his expression long enough to interpret it before Roman walked over and asked her to dance.

Ten

PARKER

P ARKER WOKE up and dressed for an early morning run along the beach. When he opened his door, he saw the outside of it had been decorated with a paper Christmas tree and decorations made out of pipe cleaners and other items left over from their craft day. For the first second, he thought maybe it was something Merit and Graham had done for everyone, but the moment he saw the sash draped on the tree that read *#1 Christmas Fan Behind this Door*, with a cat drawn curled up beneath the tree, he instantly knew it was Kelli's doing.

He stood in front of the door just smiling at it for several minutes. Then he shook his head and glanced down the hallway in the direction of Kelli's room, feeling drawn toward her at the same time he wished he had never seen Stephanie's list. Before dating his ex, he'd had all the confidence he needed, but he hadn't gotten his groove back since they had broken up. Maybe because he feared that everything on her list about him was actually true.

He had to remind himself that he was supposed to stop thinking about Kelli and headed outside. The sun hadn't risen yet, so it was still fairly dark. Even so, it was warmer than it was in Denver at midday this time of year. It was more humid here than he ever guessed it would be in December, though, and that took a bit of getting used to.

After his run, he showered and even made it down to breakfast a few minutes early.

Once he found out that they didn't need to meet for the group activity until three—serving a Christmas dinner to the homeless—he went for a walk along the boardwalk and explored the town a bit. Not that it helped to get his mind off Kelli, especially since he needed to buy a Secret Santa gift for her. Having his arm around her while they had danced last night had felt so perfectly, exactly right, that he had been afraid to dance with her a second time. It had been hard enough walking away after the first song.

He got back just a few minutes before three, afraid that if he came back any earlier, he might run into her, and he was having a hard enough time staying away. He knew he wasn't good enough for her and that he wasn't ready for another relationship.

While he waited in the family room for everyone to show up, he walked to where the points were posted. Everyone had at least four points since everyone made the ornaments and went to the dinner and dance. He had gotten his fifth point on the beach with Kelli, but several people had more than five, including Kelli, who was up to eight.

How had she gotten so many so quickly? If he didn't step it up, he was going to have to say goodbye to his parking spot for a full year.

A driver knocked on the mansion's front door not long after everyone gathered in the family room, saying he was ready to take them to the soup kitchen. They all headed outside and got in the twelve-passenger van. There were a couple of empty seats, so apparently not all of them were set on winning the prize. He purposely didn't sit next to Kelli, hoping that the distance would help his heart recover.

But once the ten of them were inside the building and got their instructions on how to help prepare the meal they would be serving to people who were homeless or otherwise struggling, he realized he wasn't going to be able to stay as far away from her as he needed. They were both put on turkey-slicing duty, working side-by-side, and he knew he couldn't bring up the dance without his feelings about the night showing as plain as day on his features, so he instead chose a safer subject.

"I see you're up to eight points now."

She smiled as she cut the meat. "And I see you're not. I think that's proof that parking spot C-seven really is mine. You might even say that it always has been."

They'd asked them to cut one-fourth inch thick slices of meat, and she cut so carefully that he thought they probably could've come along with a ruler and measured all of her slices and they'd each be exactly one-fourth an inch thick, all the way from one side to the other.

"Someone's counting their chickens. There's still a lot of week left." He didn't know why he was goading her to get more points. He really wanted that spot, but there were a lot of things on that list that he didn't want to do. And from what he'd seen at work and the fact that she was there by seven every day, he knew that she was someone who could set a goal and achieve it. He was going to have to step it up.

"Don't you worry about me. There are a lot of things on that list and a lot of hours in the day."

He moved a group of slices to the platter and turned on the electric knife again. "What did you do to earn points today?"

Her face lit up as she talked about answering letters that kids wrote to Santa, helping as an elf at the shopping center by taking pictures of kids on Santa's lap, and then wrapping gifts at a Toys for Tots charity.

Before they were finished, one of the volunteers in charge came over and asked them to move to the serving line to help the people who had just started coming in while she finished up the turkey. Because they weren't assigned which items to serve, he purposely chose a spot where there would be someone between him and Kelli.

But as he put a scoop of mashed potatoes on everyone's plates, he still found himself looking further down the line at where Kelli was placing a roll on each person's plate. She was smiling and chatting with each person. She wasn't acting like they were any less than her just because they had found themselves homeless at Christmas. The look on her face was that of zero judgment and genuine care.

He wondered if it was authentic, or if she was just very good at putting on a front. From the way everyone's faces were bright and smiley as she talked with them, they thought it was plenty genuine.

But Stephanie was pretty good at projecting the image she wanted people to see and then complaining about them afterward, and he suddenly needed to know if Kelli was the same.

After they had finished serving everyone, spent time socializing with all the people who had come to eat, and packed up the extra food in boxes for their guests to take with them, the lead organizer started assigning each of them clean-up duties. Parker took a subtle step toward Kelli, knowing that as the woman in charge reached them, she would be more likely to pair them up on a task. And she did. They both were assigned to wash the big pans.

The day had been long and exhausting—mentally and physically. Knowing that people tended to show their true colors a bit more when they were worn out, he was curious to see Kelli's. As the sinks were filling with water, she leaned against them, looking so tired. Perfect. So he asked what she thought of the people she had met. They were mostly gone, and they were far enough in the back that any that remained wouldn't be able to hear her.

Answering seemed to give her more energy. "They had so many incredible stories! Did you talk with the guy in the gray coat? He was the one wearing a beanie and mismatched boots."

"I did."

She started putting some dishes in the soapy water and washed them as she talked. "He had so many tough things happen in his life. Enough to make most people go off and be a hermit somewhere. But he was so happy and so funny. Did you see how many people he made laugh? Oh, and there was this woman who had three kids, but she'd lost custody of all of them. It was so heartbreaking to hear how sad she was around the holidays. I wanted to just wrap my arms around her and hug her for days."

As they talked, he rinsed each item as she finished, then put it in the rack, then dried and put it away while she told story after story. He was surprised that she had talked to so many people in the time they had.

Okay, all that seemed authentic. She had even talked about trying to set up rotating help from ZentCube employees at their local homeless shelter once they got back, and he had no doubt she would. But maybe that was just her thing—something that spoke to her heart.

So he searched for a different subject. Everyone had complaints about their boss, even if the boss was a great one, so he started asking about Liz. If Kelli had complaints, she didn't voice them, no matter how many opportunities he gave her.

On the ride back to the resort, he started a conversation with all ten of them in the van about things that annoyed them. Kelli did join in with her own list of annoying things, but she mentioned things like taking out her contacts at night and putting on glasses, and that the curvature of the lenses always made her question whether she was on the bottom step or still had one to go. Or thinking she had plugged in her phone to charge, then realizing that the cord wasn't pushed in all the way. Annoyances about *things*, never about *people*.

He still wasn't convinced, so he decided to check on one of the many things that really annoyed Stephanie. When they pulled to a stop light, he saw a man wearing a navy sweater and jeans walking down the street next to a woman. He hadn't known it until the end of their relationship, and had probably annoyed her countless times over the nearly two years they had dated, but Stephanie thought it was wrong and was personally offended by anyone who wore any shade of a blue shirt with blue jeans.

"See that guy?"

Kelli nodded.

"What do you think of his outfit?"

"I think he feels good in it. Look at how confident his walk is."

"But what do you think of the color of his sweater?"

She gave him an amused smile that said she knew what it was he was *really* asking. "I think that color would look great on you. Why? Did you buy one like it while you were out shopping today?"

He chuckled inside. She very much didn't understand why he was asking. He pushed further. "What do you think about it paired with jeans, though?"

He got that same amused smile from her, and she motioned at his pants. "You look mighty fine in jeans, Parker. How about the hair? I can compliment the hair, too, if you'd like."

This time, he laughed out loud. But he pushed, making sure he was specific this time. "But if you're talking style, the color of the sweater is fine when worn with jeans?"

She gave him a look that told him she was confused as to why that could possibly be something he was wondering. "I think people should wear whatever they like, especially if it makes them feel great. If whatever you're wearing makes you feel as confident as that guy looks, what you're wearing is going to look good to everyone. That's all anyone needs to worry about."

He leaned back in his seat and smiled. He might be sitting next to the least judgmental woman he'd ever known, and she'd been right under his nose for two-and-a-half years.

Eleven

KELLI

KELLI WASN'T the only one crowding around the points board in the family room before heading to the activities building to make gingerbread houses. A few people were trailing and probably had no plans to catch up. She had hoped that she was enough in the lead to skip gingerbread house making, but she was sitting at eleven points and so was Parker. And a couple of people were only one point behind them, so she couldn't risk it.

Especially because it was a two-point activity, and especially because she really, *really* wanted to win that weekly lunch for her team. And close behind that was her desire to not let Parker have her parking space for a full year.

Addison must've noticed her looking at Parker's points, because she glanced around to make sure he wasn't in the room and then said, "You work with him, right?"

Kelli shrugged. "Not really. We're in the same department but on very different teams. So I see him daily, but all along we've been rivals more than anything else." She felt like they still were, but they were also something that they weren't before, and she wasn't quite sure what exactly that was. But she found herself wanting to figure it out.

"Do you know if he's seeing someone? Or hoping to? Because he said he was single, but I'm having the hardest time getting him to pay any attention to me."

Kelli opened her mouth but had no idea what to say. Luckily, she was spared trying to come up with a reason because Addison said, "Shh. Never mind—he's coming in."

A text on her phone buzzed, so she stepped away from the points chart and to an area where she was alone and pulled out her phone. It was from Valeria.

> VALERIA: Hey, girl! How's the vacation? Full of the magic of Christmas?

> KELLI: You know it.

> VALERIA: Does that magic include a certain single man?

Her cheeks blushed just thinking about Parker before she realized that Valeria had probably been asking about Davis. She had danced with him twice more at the Tinsel and Tidings Ball, but with Parker's very timely help, Davis had seemed to understand that she didn't want anything resembling serious or exclusive, and he had backed off and just danced with her for fun. Davis really was a good guy, and at another point in her life, she would've gladly dated him and probably would have been happy. Davis was a light in the darkness.

But Parker harnessed the power of the sun, and her mind couldn't seem to do anything other than crave its brightness and warmth whenever she wasn't focused enough on what she was doing to keep her mind from wandering.

She hesitated a moment, staring at Valeria's text, before typing in, *Yes, but not the single guy you're thinking of.*

The text showed as *read* for a slight pause before she got Valeria's response.

> VALERIA: PARKER?!

> It's Parker, isn't it?

> Oh my. After all this time, it's Parker, isn't it?

> My girl has a thing for Parker Brockbank in Trade Shows!!!!

Kelli held her phone closer, glancing around to make sure no one was near enough to see.

> KELLI: Shh! I don't even know. He's just...

> And I'm...

> I know he just sees me as the awkward girl. But he's pretty great.

> And now I don't know what to do.

My current plan is to run far away.

She glanced up and saw that Parker was no longer studying the chart, and he looked like he might be doing his own running away.

KELLI: Gotta go.

"Parker," she called out, and he turned toward her. She took a few quick steps to reach him. "Where are you going?"

He glanced back at the points chart and then made a face. "I'm just not feeling like making gingerbread houses."

"I appreciate you being the gentleman and letting me win the parking space, but I would rather win it fair and square."

"I still plan to win it."

She shook her head. "You're practically gift wrapping it and putting it under the tree with my name on it if you walk out on this one."

She didn't want to go herself. And she would be fine—grateful, even—for less competition. But she wanted to win, and against her better judgment, she wanted him there, too. So she had no problem taunting her biggest rival.

He took a longing gaze at his escape route before meeting her eyes. "Okay, but only if you promise that when I win, you'll wrap it and put it under the Christmas tree with my name on it."

"Deal," she said, thrusting out her hand. He shook it, and they joined the group heading to the activities center.

Why was she doing this? She could've let him leave and stayed away herself.

But there were still the two others who were only one point behind her and Parker, and they'd pull ahead if they both didn't go.

They gathered in the activities building—eleven of them from ZentCube and fifteen or so from other parts of the resort—and a woman in her early twenties stood in front of them. "Hi, y'all! My name is HallieMae, and I've got a great activity for you today. Now as you can see, there are tables all around the room. Each spot at the tables has the same supplies—frosting and candies and a base to build your creations on. Y'all have a stack of gingerbread rectangles in front of you, and we do have some more right there in the middle of the tables in case you need them.

"At the end, we'll have a few judges we've grabbed from among our more elderly full-time residents, and we'll give awards to the tallest, the most creative, and the most beautiful. But the catch is, you only have one hour. Now go find a spot! We've got them on both sides of the table."

Kelli found a spot first and was looking at what she had to work with, organizing and straightening everything. When someone took the spot across from her, she looked up and was surprised to see Parker. Especially since there were still other open spots available.

He had seen her embarrassingly less than perfect so many times. And not just on the plane or at the dinner or doing a million little things at the mansion, but over *years*. In fact, anytime she did something embarrassing, it seemed to be when he was around to witness it. It was baffling that he sought her out.

Especially since there was a spot conspicuously open next to Addison.

Not that Kelli was complaining.

But as much as she felt herself being pulled toward Parker, a warning voice kept nagging at her, reminding her that things might not work out. She didn't have the best track record with guys, and she knew she was feeling more vulnerable than usual right now and needed to be cautious.

"Ready?" HallieMae called out. "Go!"

She smiled at seeing Parker straighten and organize all of his supplies before he got started, too.

But then she turned her focus to her gingerbread house. She had gotten the idea last year to do a standard house with a pointed roof, then have a slightly smaller house stacked on top of it, the front and back each with a triangle cut-out so it could sit nicely on it, then a third house on top that was slightly smaller than the second. Then she wanted to decorate it whimsically and fun. But an hour wasn't much time, so she'd have to work quickly.

Every once in a while, she'd glance over at Parker's creation, which looked like a cute beach cottage, and those art skills of his were definitely at work. He was working just as focused and furiously as she was.

She glanced up when his phone buzzed on the table and saw a picture of an adorable woman, with the name showing as "Mom." With as little time as they had, she figured he would ignore it and call her back later, but he didn't. He picked it up and answered as he was walking toward the other end of the big open space to chat.

Watching him compromised the time she had to work, but she couldn't help glancing up every few seconds and trying to guess how well he and his mom got along. Every time she looked, he was laughing and smiling. It might have possibly made her heart melt into a giant puddle of goo. She knew several people who had perfectly wonderful moms, and they got annoyed when she called. They didn't have a clue how lucky they were to even have a mom!

She knew she could never seriously date a guy who didn't respect his mom. He got bonus points if his mom was amazing and wonderful, and if there was a possibility that she could one day be her mother-in-law. And when that day came, she wasn't going to call her by her name—she was going to call whoever it was "Mom."

Kelli! She practically shouted to herself so she'd stop. Thinking those kinds of things, while she was watching this beautiful man she shouldn't date, seeing him smile as he put everything on hold to talk to his mom, was as good as walking right into the danger zone and completely ignoring the flashing warning lights.

So she turned all of her focus back to her gingerbread house, and before long, Parker finished his call and came back and did the same thing.

Once she got the structure all in place, she started with the decorating. For the bottom house, she decided to use the pastel-colored circular flat wafer candies as the shingles. It was her dad's favorite way to decorate the roof, so she did it to bring a little bit of him here. She put the frosting on as glue and then started placing the wafers.

As she placed the first row of shingles, her annual discussion with her dad about whether the colors should be random or done in a pattern came to mind. She let her dad win this one and placed them randomly.

With each one she placed, though, the sadness at not doing this with him started to creep in. Making gingerbread houses wasn't something she had ever done with her mom—it was something her dad had started their first Christmas without her. He said they needed to come up with some new traditions that were just for the two of them since that was their family now.

That first Christmas had been hard, and Kelli hadn't dealt with everything very well. But she and her dad creating something unique and very much them had made her feel like maybe the two of them could take on the world, as long as they had each other. She missed him.

Before she knew it, a tear was running down her cheek. She brushed it away and kept working. It felt wrong to be doing this without him. This was their thing. She and her dad together. Doing this alone wasn't right.

Not sharing all of their Christmas traditions together wasn't right.

Not spending Christmas with him wasn't right.

More tears fell. One even splashed down onto the table next to her gingerbread house.

Her dad taking off with his new family and not inviting her wasn't the same as her mom leaving. She could still text her dad, after all. But somehow that familiar grief of being left behind by a parent, of not being good enough to keep them around, settled on her and made her feel like she was going to crumble in on herself.

Her breathing quickened and hitched and she tried to keep it under control and quiet so it wasn't obvious to anyone else. Before long, she could no longer see the gingerbread house through the tears, so she hurried away in the direction of a hallway where she guessed the restrooms might be.

It had been the wrong choice. She tried the knobs on all three doors, but there weren't restrooms there—just locked storage areas. She turned to run out of the building itself if she had to and ran right into Parker's chest.

"Hey, are you okay?" He put his hands on her shoulders and pushed her back just enough to see her face. A face she very much didn't want him to see because it was tear-stained and mascara-stained and probably all red and blotchy and she knew she wasn't a pretty crier. That was why she never did it in public. But she was a mess and couldn't exactly stop the tears.

He only glanced at her face long enough to see she was upset, though, before he wrapped his strong arms around her and held her tight. She felt like she was completely falling apart, but he held her, keeping all the pieces together as she sobbed. As she grieved over the mom she lost half a lifetime ago and the dad she had been losing slowly over the past year, and then very quickly over the past week. She grieved for the scared little girl she was, the girl who couldn't seem to be perfect enough to keep either of them.

Parker didn't talk; he just held her as she silently cried, soaking the shoulder of his shirt. She felt the losses so strongly and so deeply, yet as she wept in Parker's arms, she felt more safe and protected than she'd felt in her life.

Finally, the tears ran out, and she was still in one piece. She let go of her fierce hold on him, and he loosened his arms enough that she could've stepped out of his embrace if she wanted to, but close enough that they were still there if she needed them. She wiped at the tears on her face, horrified that he was seeing how awful she must look right now.

Then she let out a breath of a laugh. "I am so sorry for doing this to your shirt." She wiped at the massive wet spot on his shirt. A wet spot that also held a good amount of mascara.

"The shirt's fine." He glanced in the direction of the main room. "There's an exit only about eight feet past the end of this hall. What do you say we get out of here?"

She nodded and wiped at the remnants of tears on her face while he went back into the main room and grabbed their jackets, then came back and held hers as she slipped her arms into the sleeves. Then she stayed tight to his side as he put an arm around her and led them outside and away from people she might see at work.

"Who do you normally spend Christmas with?" His question was soft and concerned and felt like a warm blanket on a cold day.

"My dad. He's spending this Christmas with his new wife and kids."

Parker led her through the dark and onto the lighted path that she knew would take them around the gardens and up the road to the mansion. "And I'm guessing that you normally make gingerbread houses together?"

She nodded.

"It's a tradition in my family, too. It's hard not being with them."

She looked up at him, so grateful that he understood and that he was leading her away from the crowd.

"Is your dad a Hallmark Christmas movie fan?"

She shook her head.

"Good. It's not a tradition in my family either. Watching a movie and drinking peppermint hot chocolate are both on the list—how about we head back and have a marathon? Then we won't need the two points from the group activity."

She smiled—something she wouldn't have guessed she'd feel like doing at all tonight. "Deal. But only if I get to pick the movie."

Twelve

PARKER

PARKER WOKE up to the most beautiful weather he had ever experienced over the holidays before. As much as he was dreading everything that was also a Christmas tradition for his own family, there were parts of celebrating the season that he was actually enjoying. He hadn't seen that coming.

And today, an excitement ran through everything. It was Christmas Eve, all twelve ZentCube employees were helping out at the Christmas village that ran through a huge portion of the resort grounds, and Graham was returning with his wife, Tessa, and baby Hope. The Christmas Eve dinner was tonight, and Kelli was back to smiling again.

He had been curious last night and had wanted to hear more about her family situation, but he wasn't about to ask and have her go through more grief. But as they were making hot chocolate, she told about how it had just been her and her dad growing up, and that he recently got remarried and didn't want her to spend Christmas with his new family.

And if that wasn't bad enough, she didn't have a mom. He had assumed that her mom had passed away, but then Kelli told him that she'd left them when Kelli was thirteen. When he asked, she'd said she got a birthday card from her for the first three years, but she hadn't seen her after that day, and she hadn't heard from her in ten years.

He thought back to how awkward he was at thirteen, and couldn't even imagine having one of his parents leave at that age. It had to have been devastating to her.

It made him grateful all over again that he had been lucky enough to have two parents who were both great people and who loved each other and loved him and Ethan. They had even been willing to cancel an anniversary trip that they'd been planning for decades just so he wouldn't be alone at Christmas. And knowing them, if he hadn't been invited on this trip, they might've canceled even after he told them not to.

Last night, he'd been careful to pay attention and follow Kelli's lead. As much as he would've loved to just hold her all evening, protecting her from harm, he hadn't known what she'd needed. She'd been vulnerable, and it would've felt like a violation if he just stepped in and assumed that he knew how she needed to grieve.

And, based on the movie she picked, a lighthearted, funny Christmas romance was her coping mechanism of choice. He had sat in the recliner next to her in the theater room, and they'd laughed hard and often. That laugh that he loved. That smile that he loved. That teasing back-and-forth banter that he loved.

As he had been sitting there with her, feelings he hadn't fully understood or even known he had burst to the surface. And now that they were fully noticeable, he realized that those feelings weren't new. He had been falling for her since the beginning when he first started working at ZentCube.

He'd been falling through their awkward date, through the awkwardness of working together in the weeks afterward, and through all their office pranks over the years.

He'd thought he'd pretty successfully suppressed all feelings he had for Kelli during the two years he'd been dating Stephanie, but now he wondered if, deep down, during all that time, he'd been subconsciously filing all his feelings for her in a storage box in his heart that he hadn't even known he had.

And by coming here, he had opened that box, letting his feelings for her burst free, filling him with a happiness he hadn't felt in a long time, and allowing him to fall for her completely.

Before long, they were joined in the theater room by Merit and Elise, and eventually by a handful of other ZentCube employees. With all the laughing, it felt like a party. He didn't know if Kelli was amazing at bouncing back after hard things, or if she was just excellent at putting on a happy face over inner turmoil. Whichever it was, she was a lot stronger than he had given her credit for.

The Christmas village that Elise and her team had set up was amazing. A big North Pole archway led into the village, and a train ran around the outside of the grassy area, enclosing the village within. A pathway led through a sugarplum forest, another led through Bethlehem to see a living nativity, and another led through Santa's workshop, complete with Santa and his elves at the end. There were tables with crafts, booths with food, and kids and parents everywhere.

Each of the ZentCube employees was helping with a different part of the village, and he and Kelli were, sadly, not assigned to the same place. Parker was helping get kids onto the train, letting it run around the track, then helping one group of kids unload and the next ones get on board. But from where he worked, he could see Kelli at a table, helping kids make headbands they could wear that had reindeer antlers wrapped with little blinking lights.

Just as he was getting a new group of kids onto the train, Merit, Graham, and Tessa—whom he had first met at a ZentCube Christmas party—came into the village. Graham was holding his wife's hand and cradling their baby with the other arm, looking blissfully happy.

As soon as Parker got the train started, he turned to them and said hello, shaking hands.

"Parker," Graham said, "I'd like you to meet my daughter, Hope."

"Wow," Parker said, leaning in closer to the perfect child in Graham's arms. "She is beautiful."

"Would you like to hold her?"

His eyes flew to Graham's, then Tessa's. They both looked like they were saying yes, so he looked around, hoping to find somewhere to wash his hands—he'd been around a lot of kids today—but he didn't spot anything.

Tessa opened her bag and pulled out a wipe. He quickly cleaned his hands, and then carefully cradled the baby as Graham transferred her into his arms.

The baby was sleeping, so her eyes were closed and her face was perfect and peaceful and so beautiful. Silky soft brown hair curled on top of her head, and as he cradled her in his arms, she snuggled into him. Holding her was like holding a bit of heaven.

He knew that most guys his age or younger didn't spend their time dreaming of starting a family, but Parker had been dreaming about it for a while. He couldn't wait until it was his own child he was holding. When he'd been engaged to Stephanie, he thought he'd get that chance before long. When she had broken it off, losing not just her, but the family he'd thought they'd one day have, had been hard.

But she had revealed a part of herself during the breakup that he hadn't seen before. Or that he hadn't wanted to see. He was grateful that she'd broken it off because he never would have. And now, holding this baby, it hit him all over again what a mistake marrying her would've been.

He smiled at the baby. He still hoped for this one day. There was something about holding the beautiful bundle that made him feel like any worries or troubles he had just washed away. He felt as peaceful as she looked, and he could've stood there holding her for hours. He shifted his arms a bit so he could pass her back, but when Merit stopped the train as the kids came back around and started loading and unloading the next group, he took the opportunity to hold her longer.

"You two must be in heaven every second of the day," he said, looking up at Graham and Tessa.

"We are," Graham said.

Then Graham's eyes shifted from him and baby Hope to his left, so he turned to see what had pulled Graham's attention. Kelli was watching him with a curious expression on her face. She smiled when their eyes met, and he held her gaze for a moment—long enough that he was sure that Graham would ask about the two of them, but he didn't. The man just looked down, like he was trying to hide a smile.

When Graham raised his head again, he looked to the sky. "Beautiful weather, isn't it?"

Parker nodded, keeping his eyes on the baby.

"A cold front is supposed to blow in later tonight, though, and there's a chance of snow if you can believe it. So we might get a white Christmas even on the beach."

This time Parker did look up. That was too bad; he had been hoping that Christmas would be very unlike the snow he was used to having at Christmastime.

When the train full of kids came around the second time, he figured he really should get back to work. He reluctantly passed the baby back to Graham, and the proud parents went to show off their baby to the rest of the ZentCube employees. He figured Merit would go with them, but he stayed and helped get the next group of kids onto the train.

Once the train pulled away, Merit nodded over at Kelli,

who was now fawning over the baby herself. "How are things going with you two?"

Parker flinched in surprise at the question. He hadn't realized that Merit had witnessed his silent exchange with Kelli, too. "Um, fine?"

Merit looked back at Parker. "You like her then?"

"So much more than I should."

Merit shook his head, chuckling. "Graham really does have a gift."

"What do you mean?"

"He can..." Merit looked up like he was trying to find a way to explain. "It's like he can see connections between people, even if they've never met each other. It's helpful when you're negotiating contracts with other companies, and ZentCube wouldn't be where it's at without him. But he has an uncanny ability to tell when two people have happily-ever-after potential."

Parker just stared at Merit, not fully taking in what he was trying to say.

Merit glanced toward another part of the village, smiling, and Parker suddenly wondered if that was where Elise was currently. "Graham needed to send me on vacation—long story—and he chose here because of Elise. I hadn't even met her yet, and he knew."

"That's actually pretty sweet. And helpful."

He chuckled. "Yeah. Even if it feels anything but when he makes you take a break from the company. But he didn't only do it for me. Even if you don't see all of it, he knows the people in our company pretty well, and he keeps a list of people he'd like to bring on this trip. Then he just hopes they're free over Christmas. Some of them get recommended by their managers, and some he specifically asks the managers to check on."

"He uses the Christmas trip to set people up on dates?"

"Nah. He doesn't like to meddle like that. He's always confident enough in the connection he sees that he figures all he needs to do is get the two people in a place where they can interact and magic will happen."

"And does it?"

"A lot of times, yes. It's his goal that whoever comes to this won't be alone the next Christmas. They rarely are."

Parker stared off at the ocean, blown away. "He's got that good of a track record?"

Merit nodded.

"I'm not sure why he brought *me* here, then—I'm too flawed. And I just got out of a serious relationship at the beginning of October. I'm not exactly the kind of person you can set up with someone and expect a successful happily ever after."

"Graham has had both you and Kelli on his list since last Christmas."

Parker drew back in surprise. "But he met Stephanie at the Christmas party last year. Did he not know I was engaged?"

"He knew."

Parker's eyes flew to Merit.

"You brought her to the summer social, too." Merit studied Parker's expression, which he guessed was showing something close to bewilderment. "He talked to both of you enough to know that the connection between you and her wasn't right, and he was hoping you'd figure it out before this trip." Merit studied him cautiously before carefully adding, "Because he also saw a connection that was right between you and Kelli."

Parker's mouth went dry. He tried to swallow. "I think he's wrong about me. I've got too many issues to ever be good enough for her."

The train came back around again, and Parker stopped it. He and Merit got the group of kids off and a new group on, and then started the new group around the village.

"What makes you think you're out of her league?"

He let out a huff of a humorless laugh. "My ex-fiancée spelled it out for me."

"How?"

Parker hadn't told anyone the specifics. Not Darren, not Adam, not any of his other friends, not even his parents. He had no idea why he felt compelled to tell Merit. Maybe he just needed it off his shoulders for a bit.

"She said she was just going to walk away, but she cared about me, so she gave me a list of all the ways I didn't measure up. Apparently, she'd been adding to the list from the start and, without telling me, had given me a date to overcome those flaws. The day she ended it was that date.

"I guess she should've added 'Not self-aware' to the list, because not only had I not guessed that she had a list, but I hadn't figured out what was on it, and I definitely hadn't been working on fixing them."

"Ouch," Merit said, wincing. "That's harsh. What kinds of things were on it?"

It still hurt to think about it, and he was embarrassed by every single item on it. "Some little things, like the way I pronounced some words, that I didn't have the content of the notifications on my phone hidden, that I didn't use an umbrella in the rain, that I danced in the car, some of the clothes I wore, stuff like that. And then some bigger things, like getting too focused on projects and not putting her as my number one priority."

The list was long. Some of the things he stopped doing immediately. For others, he didn't understand what he'd been doing wrong, so he'd had no idea how to fix them. Those had been the most maddening ones. The ones that brought him down the most. The ones that he didn't even let himself think about, because they stabbed him in the heart too painfully if he did.

And out of all the people he could've listed his flaws to, he couldn't believe he just told the CEO of the company he worked at.

Merit shook his head. "It sounds like a list only someone who didn't have that connection would make. I wouldn't put too much stock in it."

Merit was assuming too much. He hadn't seen the list. He hadn't seen the look on Steph's face when she'd given it to him. He hadn't heard them in her voice.

Parker had.

"Let me ask you this, then," Merit said, studying him. "Is Kelli very similar to your ex?"

Parker looked over to where Kelli held Hope, who must've woken up because Kelli was making faces at her. He watched her smiling and laughing for several long moments. Kelli was every bit as bright, happy, and nonjudgmental when she was entertaining a baby as she was talking to a stranger, a coworker, or a homeless woman.

He shook his head. She very much wasn't.

Did Graham think that Kelli would be able to look past all of Parker's faults and shortcomings and see the man who had fallen for her so completely? Maybe. He wasn't sure that Graham was correct, but he very much hoped that he was.

Thirteen

KELLI

KELLI HAD IMAGINED that the Christmas Eve dinner in the mansion would be idyllic. The sixteen of them would all eat amazing food and talk and laugh and even if you were on the outside looking in and couldn't hear what was being said, you could tell that it was a happy group, enjoying each other's company.

In a lot of ways it was. The food was fantastic and there was lots of talking and laughing. There were also hilarious stories of Christmases gone wrong, a few spontaneous bursts into song with everyone joining in, a dish of roasted butternut squash spilled, Davis and Addison looking at each other like maybe there were some sparks between the two of them, some impressions of actors in Christmas movies saying iconic lines, a couple of people who had a bit too much to drink and became quite entertaining themselves, and some sharing of favorite Christmas traditions. It felt more than idyllic; it felt like a family.

The best part, though, was sitting next to Parker through the whole thing. He was funny and sweet, and for as long as she had been working on the same floor as him, nothing at all like she had assumed. And he kept looking over at her in a way that made her heart somehow melt and do flips at the same time.

Then, Tessa told a story about how she grew up in a rural area and their family was super poor, but they decided that a neighboring family needed gifts for Christmas worse than they did. As they were sneaking across the fields to deliver them, they ran into the family they were headed toward, who just happened to be sneaking through the fields at the exact same time to give everything they had for Christmas to her family.

While Tessa told the story, Parker had his hand resting at the side of his chair and Kelli's was resting at the side of her chair. And all she could think of was how much she wanted to touch his hand. To reach out and close that distance, make that connection.

But it was scary. No, it was terrifying. What if she wasn't ready for this? What if it was a big mistake that she would regret once they got back to real life and saw each other at work five days a week?

What if he didn't want that connection? What if she reached out but was denied, and then she just ended up feeling stupid and had to find a way to avoid him for the rest of the trip?

She was feeling pulled to him so strongly, though, that she had to try. With a hand that managed to only be a little shaky, she reached across the six inches of space separating the two of them and ironically, just like in the story Tessa was telling, he was reaching across the space between them as well.

Their pinkies touched first, just brushing up against each other so softly that she held her hand there, just taking in the gentle, sweet feel of his skin barely touching hers. Then, in a burst of bravery, she linked her pinky with his.

It was such a simple thing, and it was such a small part of her that was touching him, but it was so much more than a casual or accidental brush. Their pinky fingers were entwined, *choosing* to hold onto each other.

He had caught her from falling. He had danced with her. He had held her in his arms as she cried, keeping her in one piece. Yet somehow this felt more intimate. More daring. More like a line had been crossed. A choice had been made. A choice to be reckless and brave and vulnerable and fearless.

When Tessa finished her story, Parker turned to look at her, his expression so deep and layered that she could've stared into his eyes for days trying to figure out all of it. But before she got enough of a chance, Graham clapped his hands and said, "Alright, everyone head into the family room—we're playing Christmas Charades!"

Parker and Kelli were placed on different teams, so they sat on opposite sides of the room. But she found his eyes wandering to her just as often as hers went to him. Now, though, the night felt charged, and she wondered if she was ever going to feel tired enough to head to bed. Most people seemed to feel that way, even after all the laughing from the bad acting and the hilarious guesses, so all sixteen of them played game after game, until people finally started to break away, and one by one, go to bed.

Merit walked to the windows and looked out. "I guess when we brought sixteen adults and a baby from a place as snowy as Colorado, we couldn't help but bring some snow with us."

"It's snowing?" Kelli jumped up and ran to the window, pressing her hands against the window at the sides of her face so she could see past the light in the room. "It's snowing! Is it even supposed to snow here?"

"It can sometimes," Parker said as he stepped up to her side and looked out. "Just not very often. I checked before we came."

"We should go out in it. You all brought coats, right?"

The handful of people who were still in the room looked at her with confused faces.

"You want to go out in the storm?" Graham asked.

She looked around at everyone. "Don't you all go outside whenever it storms?"

"Not if I can help it," Elise said.

Roman shook his head. "Me neither."

"But storms are so exciting." It was baffling to her that none of them raced outside whenever it rained or snowed so they could experience it in person instead of just from behind a window.

"I'll go with you."

Parker's words were as attractive as the smile on his face. She gave him a big, grateful smile back. Then she hurried up to her room to put on her coat, boots, gloves, hat, and scarf before he had a chance to change his mind. When she came back down to the main floor, he was already waiting by the door, all bundled up, and they headed outside.

The air was cold, and with each breath in, it felt like the cold was zinging into her body. In Colorado, it always seemed to warm up when it snowed. Like the clouds were a blanket in the sky, holding in all the warmth. But the wind had blown hard to bring in this storm, and it had blown all that warmth they'd felt earlier in the day to someone else. "Do you think we just got too acclimated to the warmth since we got here, and that's why the cold is such a shock?"

"Maybe," Parker said as he looked out across the ocean. "It definitely feels colder."

Kelli held her hand out to catch a snowflake as they neared the bottom of the road that their mansion was on. "Or maybe it's just because this snow is wetter."

"Are you cold? Because we can head back."

"I'm fine. Unless you're cold?"

He smiled at her in a way that made her warm down to her toes. She would be just fine out here as long as she was with Parker. "I'm fine, too. But we could just watch the storm from the balcony at the mansion. That way we'd be close if things get too cold."

"No, because look!" Kelli pointed to the main resort area as it came into view. "Look at all the Christmas lights! Oh, it's so beautiful. We *have* to go see them in the snow."

The Christmas village was completely lit up in colorful lights, and so were all the buildings and pathways, even more than they had been when they'd gone to the dance. Every building and the trees and pathways around it were lit up in a different color, so one building was all purple, one was all green, one was blue, one was red, and one was white. An archway of lights went down the main pathway, each arch a different color, making a rainbow. It was the most incredible display of lights she had ever seen.

And with the snow falling, all the lights seemed to twinkle, like a magic spell had been cast over the whole resort. "I am so sad for everyone who stayed back in the mansion."

Parker looked at her, smiling, and she thought it was possibly the most amazing smile she had ever seen. She snuggled in close to him as they walked down the first pathway of lights, and he wrapped an arm around her, keeping her warm and protected. She hadn't even thought about snuggling into him before she did it—it had just seemed so natural. Maybe all her fears had just been stupid excuses to not be brave.

It wasn't like she had the best track record when it came to dating, though. She usually just went with what made her heart happy and kept logic out of it. She was trying to use logic this time around, and logic told her that she shouldn't be dating someone who could make things awkward at work.

It told her that she shouldn't be dating *anyone* right now. She knew that a man with a great family was her kryptonite, and with things being so unsettled with her dad, she knew her heart was extra unprotected. She needed to keep it far from danger, not snuggle up to danger.

So she ran. A bunch of pathways converged in one big open crossroads, with lights twisting up the five street lamps surrounding the area. She just needed to put a teeny bit of space between them, and she hoped Parker saw it as her running to the magical spot instead of running from him. She put her arms straight out and turned around in a slow circle, her face turned up at the sky, soaking in the beauty of the meandering snow falling softly on her, the lights casting a warm glow on everything.

She stopped turning and looked at Parker, who was looking at her with the same expression that she'd just had as she'd marveled at the lights and snow. It made her want to go to him. To snuggle into him. Maybe she didn't need to run from danger. Maybe all she needed was to know what her weaknesses were, to be cautious when it came to them, and to be brave when it came to everything else.

Because this man smiling at her from a dozen feet away was so very perfect.

A loud crack sounded off in the distance. The lights all over the resort shut off at once, plunging everywhere into darkness, and Kelli screamed. She hadn't even noticed there was a new moon until she didn't have even its light. And with the clouds from the snowstorm covering the sky, even the light from the stars was hidden. The silence was everywhere.

She wasn't afraid of the dark.

But this wasn't the dark. This was the absence of everything, including sounds. It made her feel as though there wasn't anything around her. Like everything had fallen away, leaving her drifting and alone with nothing to hold on to, nothing to ground her. "Parker?" she called out, her heart racing as she shuffled forward, hands out, desperate to grasp hold of anything. She wished she had brought her cell phone so she would have her own source of light.

"I'm here. I'm coming."

Hearing his voice helped her to slow her panicked breathing. She hoped that her heart would take the hint and calm down, too, but it didn't.

Parker must've pushed a button to light up his watch because she could suddenly see a faint light heading toward her. The light was enough to give her something to fix her eyes on, making it feel like she wasn't alone in a void. She stopped moving her arms in front of her, frantic to find something to grasp, and just kept her eyes on the light as it bobbed its way toward her.

And then Parker was there and she grabbed hold of him tight, pulling herself into that strong chest of his, and a peace washed over her. He wrapped his arms around her, rubbing the middle of her back in calming strokes. She felt safe in his arms, and this time, both her breathing and her heart started to calm.

"It's unnerving. I know. But I'm sure they'll have backup generators going soon. There will be enough light to find our way back before long."

She nodded and laid her head on his chest as the snow fell all around them in the complete darkness, wishing she could hear the comforting sound of his heart through his coat. But she could hear his breathing, and that was enough.

She was so grateful that he was so quick to help, so good at comforting her, and so sweet and thoughtful. He was a source of light all on his own.

For so long, she hadn't let herself notice all of the good things about him. At first, it had been out of fear that things would be even more awkward at work than they'd been after their first disastrous date. Then it had been because they had both started dating other people. They'd both been single for a while now, but she'd still held back out of fear that her heart couldn't handle being open to the risks again.

He moved one of his arms that had been on her back to her side and said, "Will you tap my watch?"

She reached a gloved finger up and gave his watch a tap, lighting up the screen and illuminating his beautiful face as a smile spread across his lips.

"Merry Christmas, Kelli Ellis."

"It's after midnight?" He nodded, and she smiled so big that she felt it breathe excitement into her whole body. "Merry Christmas, Parker Brockbank."

She had gotten to know and admire him here so much more deeply than she ever had at work. She had seen the goodness in him. As he held her in the darkness, the two of them seeming to be the only things that existed, she realized that when they got back to the office, things *couldn't* be the same. They had already both been changed too much to ever go back to the way they were.

So maybe there wasn't harm in moving forward. She knew her heart needed protecting, but Parker had shown that he was pretty good at protecting her when she was most vulnerable—maybe she could trust him with her heart, too.

A hum sounded in the distance, followed closely by the buzz of the streetlights above. Only every third light turned on, and only at a fraction of its usual brightness, but it was enough to show that things other than the two of them existed. Enough to show the faint outline of Parker's face.

And enough to show a sparkle of light in his eyes as he looked at her. At her back, his arms shifted as he pulled one glove off. Then he brought his bare hand to her face, wiping a few melted snowflakes from her forehead and temple with his fingertips. His hands were so warm and soft and gentle, and as his fingers got to her cheeks, she leaned into them, soaking in his touch.

Then she took off one of her gloves and reached her warm hand up to his face. She brushed her palm against his neck, her thumb resting just in front of his ear, her fingertips finding their way under his hat and into his hair.

Linking pinkies with him at dinner had felt bold and risky. As her eyes went back and forth between his eyes and the faint outline of his lips in the darkness, the thought of kissing him felt so far beyond bold and risky that she was afraid she would back out.

Except it also felt so right.

And from the way he was looking at her, she could tell that it felt right to him, too.

So she rose on her toes slightly and pulled him toward her with both the hand on his neck and the hand clutching onto the coat at his chest. He responded by wrapping his warm hand around the back of her neck and pulling her closer at the waist.

She pressed her lips against his, soft and careful. As they kissed, their cold noses brushed each other's cheeks, but their lips warmed quickly. He let out a whisper of a groan, and she melted into him, loving that their kiss was having as strong of an effect on him as it was on her.

Everything in the world seemed to fade around them, but instead of it being terrifying like when the power had first gone out, this time it made her feel like she had everything she needed right there in her little bubble.

He deepened the kiss, and she knew she was a goner. She was handing him her entire heart, and he was putting his strong hands around it, keeping it safe.

Fourteen

PARKER

PARKER WOKE to the sound of Graham and Merit strolling down the hallways, singing a very loud and very off-key rendition of *We Wish You a Merry Christmas* as they knocked on everyone's doors. Parker rolled over to look at the alarm clock on his bedside table, but apparently, the power was still out. He picked up his phone—which he'd plugged in, but was now down to ten percent power—and saw that it was barely seven a.m. Five a.m. Denver time.

He pushed his phone into the pocket of his pajamas because his parents hadn't known when they'd be on shore and available to call, and he didn't want to miss it. Then he took a look outside. It was still dark and everything was wet and very cold-looking, but it was beautiful. And not exactly the white Christmas Graham had been rooting for.

He headed downstairs with every other bleary-eyed ZentCube employee, most of whom had blankets wrapped around their shoulders and shuffled more than walked. He was used to waking up at five-thirty Denver time, so this wasn't too far out of the ordinary, but he also never went to bed as late as he had last night if he had work the next day.

They all gathered in the family room around the tree. As soon as he saw Kelli and the way her face lit up as soon as she saw him, he decided that any amount of sleep deprivation was just fine with him if it involved being able to see her.

The sun hadn't risen yet, but Graham and Merit had placed dozens of candles around the room. He couldn't take his eyes off Kelli, marveling at how beautiful she looked in the golden glow of the candles. He wished he could place kisses on those beautiful lips, on her temples, and all along that beautiful jawline.

Instead, as he stepped up to her, he reached for her hand, brought it to his lips, and brushed kisses across her knuckles. She closed her eyes and sighed. Maybe believing in the "magic of Christmas" wasn't something just for childhood.

"Sit down, sit down," Graham said. "Everyone find a seat."

Parker sat down next to Kelli on one of the couches and listened as Merit told a story about his childhood Christmases. They had been super poor, and any presents they got were inexpensive. So his mom had started a tradition of going around and having everyone say what they were grateful for before opening anything. By the time they had all finished, they felt like they already had everything they could want. So the presents were just icing on the cake and they were always happier with Christmas than any of their friends—even the ones who got everything they had wished for.

As they went around the circle, each person saying what they were grateful for, he thought about how much he had been dreading this Christmas, and how it had turned out so much better than he could've ever hoped. He had a lot to be grateful for.

Including last night. He'd wanted to kiss Kelli for quite a while, but he had wanted that moment to be perfect for her. He never would've chosen their first kiss to be in the freezing cold, their coats and shoes getting soaked, with the power out, scaring her. But even with all that, it had ended up being perfect after all. There may not have been electricity at the resort, but he had felt electricity coursing through him plenty.

The kiss had blown his mind. Never had a kiss felt like that before. As they had stood there in their winter gear and he held her close, everything fell away, all his worries and cares, and all that was left was a beautiful woman who was more amazing than he'd ever known, who seemed to want to be with him as much as he wanted to be with her.

His imagined perfect evening with her also would've included an unseasonably warm night, a clear sky full of stars, and Christmas lights surrounding them. But they had found a bench and sat down in the near darkness and enjoyed a peaceful silence that could only come from a power outage and falling snow, her head against his shoulder and his arm around hers. They had talked for hours on that bench, and he couldn't think of anything more perfect. And he couldn't imagine himself falling more fully for anyone.

But now that it was morning, fears started settling in. He wanted things to work out between him and Kelli more than he'd ever wanted it with anyone else. And things were going so well between the two of them. But he had thought that things were going well between him and Stephanie, too, so he didn't trust that he could tell when things were going well or not.

As it came time to open Secret Santa presents, Merit and Elise sat next to the tree and started handing them out, one at a time. After a handful of people opened their presents and then found out who their Secret Santa was, more often than not it was from someone each person had clearly shown signs of liking throughout their trip.

When Thomas stopped grinning enough that he could talk after opening a Chia Pet that was a sculpture of Bob Ross and finding out it was from Joy, he said, "I'm having a hard time believing that the names we drew for Secret Santas were random."

"No, at one point they were," Graham said, "I swear. Carla gave me the random list. And then I shifted things around just a bit when I thought it might be more...beneficial for someone to try to get to know someone else a little better." The man just grinned unapologetically for switching around names.

Parker wondered if his Secret Santa had been selected by Graham, or if it had been random. He had gotten Kelli's name, and with what Merit had told him at the

Christmas Village, he assumed it wasn't random. He wasn't all the way sure, though, until Elise handed him a package and the wrapping paper on it was of cats, all wearing Santa hats. He laughed out loud and looked at Kelli as soon as he saw it.

He carefully took off the paper and opened the box. A shirt was folded in an exact rectangle, with a handwritten paper on top that was so perfectly written it could've been a font. He read it out loud. "I'll tell you right now that you will look great in this. Paired with jeans that you also look great in. And your hair looks pretty fantastic, too." And, of course, the shirt was blue.

Kelli hadn't known the significance behind the shirt, which made it mean even more to him. He smiled at her, and said, "Thank you," and she grinned back until Elise handed her a gift. Then she looked at it with curiosity, and he was suddenly nervous.

But he loved the sound of her laugh when she saw the wrapping paper. He'd been so excited when he found the paper at a gift shop on the Boardwalk. It was silver and gold and sparkly, so it kind of fit the Christmas theme, but it was probably meant to wrap a New Year's gift because it was covered in glasses of champagne. They weren't water goblets, exactly, but he'd gotten a Sharpie and personally drawn a mushroom at the bottom of every glass.

She unwrapped the gift and lifted the lid on the box. He watched her face closely as she picked up the paper where he had written, "For next time, when we continue our new Christmas tradition." Then, still holding the paper in one hand, she lifted the "Hallmark movie-watching blanket" out of the box and hugged it to her chest.

He had sat at the desk in his room for a long time, pen hovering over the paper, trying to figure out what he wanted to write, and then being nervous about writing something so bold and presumptive. Eventually, he just did it and hoped for the best. By the heart-stopping way she was looking at him now, he'd made the right choice.

Not long after the last present was opened, he felt the buzz of a text and pulled out his phone, expecting it to be from his parents or his brother, but it was from his friend, Josh.

> JOSH: Hey, buddy! Merry Christmas!

> I was just thinking of you, and wondering if you're leaning one way or another on that job offer. I would love to start working with you again.

> No pressure. You have until New Year's to decide, of course. I'm just curious.

Parker excused himself and headed away from the group in the family room and found a seat in the living room at the front of the mansion, trying to figure out how to respond to the text. He hadn't spent much time even thinking about it while they'd been on this trip. Before he left, he had been seriously considering taking the job. Josh was a good friend, and it would be great to work with him again. And it was a great offer.

Although he hadn't put a ton of thought into it, he

knew himself well enough to know that his loyalties lay with ZentCube. And whenever the job offer did happen to cross his mind while he'd been at The Royal Palm, all he could think of was Kelli. He had spent two years and seven months working on the same floor as her as co-workers and occasional pranksters. How great would it be to see her daily as they dated?

He took a moment to imagine it, his smile growing bigger the longer he pictured it.

But what if he messed things up? What if he hadn't been ready to start dating again like Darren thought he was? What would happen when she discovered all the negative things about him that Stephanie had discovered?

By that same token, how awful would it be to see her daily if things didn't work out between them? Sure, they had known each other for quite a while, but their relationship was new. There were so many ways he could screw it up, and it didn't matter how awkward their first date was and the months working together following it—that would be nothing compared to how awful it would be to see her daily if they broke up.

He knew her now. He loved her now. He wasn't the same person who had shown up at the airport last Saturday morning. Even the thought of their relationship not working out felt like a stab in his chest. He wasn't sure he could fully comprehend how painful it would be to see her daily if they broke up.

Maybe getting this other job offer right now, where he not only got to spend the equivalent of a month and a half dating Kelli during a single week, but he got space to decide if the job change was right, was some divine timing. He took a deep breath and then responded to the text.

> PARKER: There are a lot of things keeping me at ZentCube.
>
> A lot of people, too. One in particular.
>
> I'm not ready to say no to your company's offer yet, though. I just need to see how a few things here work out first.
>
> JOSH: Ahh. I understand. No worries. You've got time to figure it out.
>
> And remember that I'm happy to answer any questions, anytime.
>
> Or do anything else I can to sway you to join our team, especially since you have so many things swaying you in ZentCube's direction.
>
> PARKER: Thanks, Josh.

Parker put his phone back in his pocket and hoped—even made a Christmas wish—that he would be able to turn down Josh's job offer. Because nothing would make him happier than spending every day at ZentCube with Kelli.

Fifteen

KELLI

Kelli admired the impossibly soft blanket that Parker had given her as she took it up to her room, folded it neatly, placed it at the bottom of her bed, and put his note on the nightstand. She was still on a high from their kiss last night and from their conversation on the bench. It had felt like a magical place where the two of them were the only people in the world, and they had all the time they wanted to just talk about everything.

The more she learned about Parker and the more time she spent with him, the more in love she fell.

Around the Christmas tree, she had caught him looking at her several times, and the look on his face was so sweet that it had made her heart do little leaps of joy. It was still doing little leaps of joy.

Someone yelled, "The power's back on!" and even though she could hear the hum of electricity, she still ran to the light switch in her room and turned it on just to check.

Yes! It really was. Her phone was still plugged in and sitting on her nightstand from last night. It had died before the power went out, but she hadn't made it upstairs to plug it in before they'd gone outside to enjoy the storm. She had hoped that the power would come on during the night and she'd wake up with a charged phone, but of course, it hadn't.

She sat on the bed, trying not to bounce in anticipation as she waited for it to charge enough to power back on. It took *forever*. After a minute or two, she checked to make sure that the cord was plugged in tight to her phone. It was. And then another minute or two later, she checked behind the nightstand to see if it was plugged tightly into the wall. It was.

Finally, the screen lit up as it booted back to life. There were probably going to be about a million messages from her dad, telling her Merry Christmas, asking her how things were going, and wondering why she wasn't responding to his texts. She couldn't wait to tell him all about the retreat and all about Parker.

But when the lock screen finally appeared, she only found one text—a video from her dad. He was in his suite in whatever Cabo San Lucas hotel he was staying in, an explosion of wrapping paper all around him.

"Hi, Sweetheart! Merry Christmas! I hope you've been having a blast on your trip. Sorry, I don't have time to chat—JoAnn and the girls have our day packed so full—but I'll call in a day or two. In the meantime, you keep living it up in Myrtle Beach and soaking in that sun. Talk soon. I love you."

He didn't have time to chat for even a couple of

minutes. She didn't respond to the text. She took a slow, deep breath then placed her phone back on her nightstand and walked out of her room.

As she was walking past Parker's room on her way back downstairs, he called out through his partially open door, "Hey, Kelli, wait!"

She paused, and he was at his door in a flash. "I'm video chatting with my family, and they want to meet you. What do you say?"

She should say no. Family was her weakness, and she knew it. But she was so curious about his, and she wanted to learn everything there was to know about him. Family was a big part of who a person was; how was she supposed to get to know him without getting to know his family? She should meet them.

No, you shouldn't, a voice said. But she reminded the voice that everything was okay, as long as she recognized her weakness and was cautious about it.

Besides, she was falling hard for Parker, and she really wanted to. And all she had gotten from her dad was a seventeen-second video text, so she felt a little cheated and was very much craving a family chat.

She smiled, said yes, and went into his room to where a laptop was open on his desk, showing three faces smiling at her. Parker offered her the desk chair and dragged over an armchair for him to sit next to her.

"Kelli, I would like you to meet my mom, Jessica, my dad, Bennett, and my brother, Ethan. Everyone, this is Kelli Ellis."

His mom had the same dark eyes and hair, only with grays throughout that looked elegant on her. And she had crow's feet at the sides of her eyes like she was a woman used to smiling. Kelli liked her instantly. His dad had lighter brown hair, but the same strong jawline and strong shoulders as Parker's. And his little brother was adorable. Like he was just as used to getting into good-natured mischief as he was to helping old ladies carry their groceries.

"Oh my goodness," his mom said. "Parker told us you were beautiful, but that was an understatement."

Kelli knew she was blushing. So much heat rose to her cheeks that they must be bright red.

His dad nodded. "He also tells us that you are smart, creative, talented, and dedicated, and that ZentCube wouldn't be as successful as it is if it weren't for you and your marketing skills."

She looked over at Parker and saw that he was blushing, too, and looking down to hide it. It was so cute.

They started by asking questions about her, but they all seemed to enjoy chatting, so she started asking them questions about them and about Parker. Then they were all just chatting about random things—their three different trips, how Ethan was liking school, what his parents did for a living, favorite Christmas traditions—all five of them.

She had thought she would be in his room for five minutes or less, but before she first even thought about what time it must be, a good half an hour had already passed.

As they said their goodbyes, Kelli realized she was falling in love with the whole family, and as she was getting ready for their carriage ride later that evening, she felt like she was floating.

By the time they walked out front to meet their carriages, she had to remind herself to pull her heart back and give some space between it and Parker's family. Without even realizing she had done it, she had fallen in love with James because of his family, and she didn't want to do the same thing ever again. And she knew that right now she was especially vulnerable since she was feeling particularly lacking in the family department.

Four beautiful horse-drawn carriages were waiting outside, majestic horses at the front of each, standing tall and occasionally pawing a hoof on the wet road or making a snorting sound. There were spots for four people per carriage, so Parker and Kelli sat in the back seat in one carriage and Joy and Thomas sat in the seat facing them.

"They have blankets for us, too," Kelli exclaimed, pulling theirs up to her shoulders and snuggling up to Parker. He put an arm around her shoulders, so she reached up and adjusted the blanket so it would go over her shoulder enough to cover his arm. It wasn't as cold as last night, but it wasn't the warm weather they'd had the first few days, either.

As the carriages pulled away and started heading down the road, Joy said, "I can't believe they are awarding points to us for this. I don't know about you guys, but I didn't need to be bribed."

Parker chuckled. Kelli was sitting close enough to him that she could feel his laugh rumble in his chest. "Even the people who have no chance of winning are here, so I think you might be on to something."

"Who do you think's going to win?" Joy asked.

"Me," both Kelli and Parker said at the same time. They all laughed, and so did she, but it wasn't a joke—she was still determined to win.

Thomas tapped a finger to his bottom lip. "So you're saying I should either kick it in high gear or just accept the fact that I'm not going to win."

Kelli liked Joy and Thomas. And by how close they were sitting, they liked each other, too. Maybe she and Parker could go on double dates with them once they were back in Denver.

Her stomach fluttered at the thought of her and Parker dating when they got back. Everything here felt like a magical dream—one that would disappear and be forgotten once they left. But it wasn't. She was going to be able to see Parker every day at work. After their hours of chatting on the bench in the snow last night, she knew that was what they both wanted.

But what if she wasn't as ready to head into another relationship as she had thought she'd been last night? Her fluttery stomach turned into a quivering one.

Then Parker pulled her in a little closer as they went over a little bump when the carriage turned off The Royal Palm's property and onto the streets of Myrtle Beach. She just fit so well next to him. And he was so kind and chivalrous. Any time she saw him, her entire body felt like it was filled with twinkle lights and Christmas magic. Maybe she was ready after all.

As they drove through the streets of Myrtle Beach, looking at all the Christmas lights stretched across the main streets and decorating the buildings, Kelli laid her head against Parker's shoulder. He had unzipped his coat, so apparently he was plenty warm with just the blanket. She put her hand right over his heart, feeling the strong, steady rhythm of his heartbeat.

He kissed her forehead, and when she looked up at him and smiled, he said, "Stay until New Year's Day with me."

She sat up straight so she could get a better look at him. "You've decided to stay?"

He reached out a hand and brushed a lock of hair off her cheek, then ran his fingers down her cheek, across her jaw, and stopped at her chin, using one finger to trace her lips. His touch sent electricity zinging through her and made her long to have his lips on hers again.

"If I could stay here with you forever, I would."

She was so hopelessly gone at his words. She just stared into those dark eyes with the honey color nearest his pupils and forgot how to speak. How to think. How to do anything but fall into their depths.

He cupped his fingers under her chin and leaned forward to brush his lips against hers and then smiled, showing a dimple that she loved so much. With his lips only an inch from hers—close enough that she could feel each beautiful breath—he whispered, "Is that a yes?"

She laughed, realizing that she hadn't managed to get an

answer out. "Yes, Parker. I would love to stay here with you until the very moment they kick us out."

She felt a buzz in her coat pocket and jumped before she remembered that she had brought her phone along just in case her dad got a chance to call or text. She pulled it out and looked at the screen, surprised that it was someone other than him.

It was a text from James's sister Catherine, the sister that she had gotten closest to while she had dated James. The text simply said, *I MISS SEEING YOU AT FAMILY THINGS*.

She tried to push down the memories of good times with Catherine and James's family that the text brought back, and shoved the emotions right along with them. She'd try to respond later, but she couldn't now. She pushed the phone back into her pocket.

Parker looked at her, concern all over his face. "Are you okay?"

What was she doing? She had let herself bond with James's family, so she knew first-hand how painful it was to get close to a boyfriend's family, knowing that if you ever broke up with the boyfriend, you could never see his family again.

She was trying to not let herself fall for Parker so quickly and so fully and so completely. But it was *Parker*. And the man was just way too easy to fall for. She still had no idea how she had worked on the same floor as him for two-and-a-half years without falling blindly, madly, fully in love with him.

"I'm great," she said and flashed him a big smile.

Sixteen

PARKER

Parker woke up happy before his brain was even awake enough to remember why he was so happy. The carriage ride last night had been so amazing, and he'd spent the whole time memorizing how it had felt to have Kelli in his arms. To have her head on his shoulder, her breath on his neck.

He picked up his phone to text her good morning and hoped a little that maybe there would be a text from her. Instead, his screen was filled with social media notifications. He just stared at them, confused, not understanding why so many random comments were showing up on his screen. He tapped on one of them.

And then he wished he hadn't. They were all comments on a post that his ex-fiancée had made. He scrolled up to Stephanie's post, dreading reading it, but feeling like he needed to know what was going on.

Hey, everyone! You all know that my wedding with Parker Brockbank was supposed to be last week. I've had quite a few people check in to ask about it, so I thought I'd give an update. Most of you know that Parker and I called off our wedding a few months ago. I know. But don't go clicking on that sad emoji, because there's no reason to feel bad for me. I'd like to announce that I've met the most wonderful man on the planet. His name is Roger, and I feel so blessed to be adored by him. Sometimes we have to go through the pain of a catastrophic hurricane to get to the sunshine and blue skies and true love on the other side.

The picture she posted with it was of her and Roger on vacation together, and it looked like they were on one of the islands his honeymoon cruise with her was supposed to stop at. And now she was there with her "true love," and feeling blessed that she was no longer with Parker, her "catastrophic hurricane."

And of course, she had tagged him in her post. That way he was sure to also see all the comments from her friends—people he used to call friends, too—about how she shouldn't feel bad because Parker wasn't good enough for her, and how glad they were that she had found someone better.

He un-tagged himself from the post and closed out of the app, his teeth grinding and all the muscles in his body tensing. Instead of heading straight to the shower as he'd planned, he got dressed in his gym clothes and shoes and took off for a run along the beach. He needed to do something constructive with his racing heartbeat so he didn't do something stupid instead.

But running gave him too much time to think and question if he ever was or ever could be relationship material. Stephanie certainly didn't think so. Dozens of people commenting on Stephanie's post didn't seem to think he was, either. And they were mostly people he had known. People who hadn't given him any kind of indication that they thought he wasn't worthy of Stephanie.

What made him think he could start a new relationship and be successful? Especially with someone as incredible as Kelli?

Even after showering, he still couldn't shake the weight he'd been carrying since reading Stephanie's post. Running usually helped, but since it hadn't, he didn't know what else to try. So even though he didn't feel like it, he met up with everyone else in the family room to go make snowmen out of sand. It didn't sound possible, but maybe it had a chance of distracting him.

When he walked into the family room, though, his eyes immediately found Kelli, and her face lit up again just from seeing him. He couldn't let Stephanie bring him down. Not when a relationship with Kelli was on the line. *Kelli is different*, he told himself. *You are different.*

Since the storm passed, the weather climbed back into the sixties, and with the sun shining, the beach felt amazing. As it turned out, it wasn't impossible to distract himself when Kelli was around, and it also wasn't impossible to make a snowman out of sand. It just involved creative stacking and packing of wet sand, the same way making a castle did. They were just making a "castle" that was taller than he'd ever made, so it took some extra good packing, which they'd found out the hard way. Joy and Thomas were working with them, and for the most part, they were having fun.

But something seemed off with Kelli, and his mind never drifted far from that fact. She wasn't smiling as easily as normal, and when he asked her if she was okay, she responded with "I'm fine." He was pretty sure that meant she was anything but fine. Maybe she had been coming up with her own list of things about him that annoyed her. Every time he worried about her even for a second, the weight of Stephanie's post settled on him again.

They needed some wetter sand, so when Kelli grabbed a bucket and said she'd get some, he grabbed a bucket and said he would, too. Once they were away from everyone else, he said, "It seems like something is bothering you. Do you want to talk about it?"

She glanced toward everyone who was busy working in groups of four to make their snowmen, as if she was making sure they couldn't hear, then let out a huge breath. "I logged in to work, just to check the numbers from my campaign that was running over Christmas. Now don't give me any grief about being a workaholic, because you put in as many hours at the office as I do, and I haven't logged in the whole time we've been here."

She shook her head, looking down at the bucket she was shoveling sand into. "I don't even know what made me log in this morning. I've been enjoying the trip and hadn't even thought about work most days. I guess I was just feeling worried or unsettled or something, and I kind of just wanted that boost you get from seeing a job you worked hard on doing well, you know?"

He nodded. He knew exactly what she meant—it was one of the reasons why he was a workaholic, too.

She glanced up, looking even more worried that someone might hear, her cheeks flushing. Then she whispered, "It's going terribly, Parker. So, so, so bad. I made a huge mistake and wasted a big chunk of our marketing budget. Liz probably doesn't even know about it yet, but when she finds out, she's going to fire me."

"She's not going to fire you."

"She is! I took a big risk, thinking it was going to go well and knock everyone's socks off, and it tanked. And then after she fires me, Graham and Merit are going to find out and they're going to wish they never brought me on this trip."

"Kelli." He held onto her hand and pulled her to standing. "She's not going to fire you. Taking risks is a good thing, especially with your record. Taking risks is also what gives the biggest return on investment. Liz doesn't expect every risk to pay off." Even as he said the words, he hoped that she would be willing to keep taking risks—like taking a risk on him, specifically.

"I've been trying to be the perfect, model employee because I really like working at ZentCube, and that mistake showed that I'm the exact opposite of a perfect, model employee. I'm not even sure if winning a weekly lunch for my team for a year is going to make up for a mistake that huge."

The skin just under her eyes was turning pink, and he could tell by her erratic breathing that she was on the verge of tears but didn't want to cry with everyone around. He wrapped his arms around her, enveloping her in a hug.

"Kelli, Liz has been your boss for how long now?"

"Two years and nine months."

"Which has been plenty of time for her to witness your marketing skills. Besides, didn't she have to sign off on the ad? She's not going to fire you over bad numbers on one campaign when she's seen everything you can do."

"Do you really think so?"

"I'm positive. Everything is going to be just fine."

She breathed out a huge breath and then looked up at the sky, probably trying to convince her tears to go away. After a moment, she looked back at him and smiled before she gave him a quick peck on the lips. "I don't know if it's going to be fine or not, but thank you, Parker."

He kissed her forehead and then crouched down with her to finish filling the buckets. He knew this had been a difficult thing for her to share, and he liked that she was willing to share it with him.

But at the same time, it also felt like a test. Like maybe she shared with him to see how he would react to finding out she wasn't perfect, and he wasn't sure if he passed. Whether or not she was perfect had nothing at all to do with how much he loved her. He wasn't sure he got that across at all. Or if he had comforted her in the way he should have. His mind had been so much on his own issues that he was no longer sure.

Seventeen

KELLI

KELLI WENT to bed feeling like she had a lump of coal in the pit of her stomach, and she woke up feeling exactly the same. She kept checking her email on her phone, expecting one to come in from Liz at any moment that told her that she'd really messed up and that they needed to talk about her future at ZentCube as soon as she was back in town.

And to top that off, their group activity had been to bake cookies during the afternoon, and then go Christmas caroling down the halls of the main Royal Palm Resort guest quarters, singing and delivering cookies to anyone who opened their door to listen to them sing.

All of that would've been fine, except that she had tripped on a rug and fell into Parker, spilling her plate of cookies on the floor.

Then, she sang the wrong verse of a song, and when she tried to correct it, the words of both songs mixed and came out completely wrong and very inappropriately, much to the delight of most of the ZentCube employees around her and the older gentleman they were singing to, and to the horror of the man's wife.

And if that wasn't enough, things only got worse when she and Parker went on an actual date to The Green Olive, the fancy restaurant at the resort. She had left for the restroom when they had first arrived, just after the nice man, Declan, had shown them to their seats.

While she was walking back, she stepped wrong on her heel, twisting her ankle. It hurt pretty badly, but she wasn't about to let Parker know of one more thing she messed up on. A table with four women about her age had front-row tickets to her missed step, so she just smiled at them, and then walked the rest of the way to her table, pretending her ankle was fine.

Within moments of sitting down, their waiter brought a cocktail drink to Parker and said, "This is from the ladies at that table right over there."

Parker turned to look at the women who had just witnessed her twisted ankle and were now looking somewhat embarrassed that they just sent a drink to a man who was on a date. Well, at least three of them were. The fourth made her hand into a phone and mouthed, "Call me."

And then, the cherry on top of the cake was actually a stuffed cherry tomato they'd gotten as an appetizer. She laughed at one of Parker's jokes at the worst time, causing her to choke on the tomato just as she had put it in her mouth. And choked badly enough that Parker had to do the actual Heimlich maneuver just so she could breathe.

She had never had so many embarrassing, less-than-perfect moments with one person before. Especially not within a time frame of less than three hours.

No, she had once before. But the last time that many things had gone wrong on a single date, Parker hadn't asked her out again for two-and-a-half years.

When it came time to leave, she realized that although her ankle wasn't badly damaged and would probably be fine in a day or two, it still hurt too badly to walk back to the mansion in four-inch heels. So she had to tell Parker about it after all. He was so sweet about it—he asked the host if he could arrange to have a golf cart drive them back to the mansion, and he even picked her up and carried her to the golf cart and set her down ever-so-gently on it like she was a princess and he was her prince.

But still, she had worried all the way back to the mansion that he must've been thinking that he should've never asked her on the date.

They got back just in time to take a slow breath and grab some ice for her ankle before they met with everyone else at nine p.m. in the family room. "Welcome to our final gathering for this retreat!" Graham said.

They all cheered, and Kelli looked around at the group, feeling a sentimental longing for the group even though they were still together. After spending so many hours a day together for so many days in a row, they were feeling like family, and she was sad to see it come to an end.

"Please correct me if I'm wrong, and I do mean please correct me, because if I am, then your plane tickets are wrong. Most of us are leaving tomorrow on the ten a.m. flight back to Denver. The people who took us up on our offer to stay until New Year's Day are Parker, Kelli, Addison, Davis, and Merit. And I think we all need to cheer for that last one because he's such a workaholic; you wouldn't believe what I had to do to bribe him to come on vacation here during the summer."

Everyone laughed and cheered, then Graham said, "Actually, Elise, stand up. This is who we really should be cheering for, or we probably wouldn't have seen Merit here for more than two or three days. She's in charge of the New Year's Eve celebration here, and since she's here, Merit's here."

Elise stood up as they all clapped and whooped, her cheeks blushing, but then she looked at Merit and Merit looked at Elise and Kelli sighed. The looks they gave each other were just so sweet and so like the looks she had been getting from Parker. At least they were before her disastrous last couple of days. She chanced a glance at Parker, and he responded by entwining his fingers in hers and giving her hand a little squeeze, which warmed her heart.

And also surprised her a bit. She figured he would be trying to back away by now. She hadn't been good enough for her mom to stay, for her dad to want her in his new family, and probably to keep her job at ZentCube. And she hadn't been good enough for a brand new relationship to take hold. Maybe Parker was backing away, and the hand squeeze was just his way of letting her down very gently. That would be a very Parker thing to do.

Davis and Addison seemed happy to be having their own little love story going on, though. After the awkwardness at the dance, things had gone back to being easy between Davis and Kelli. And since he hadn't spent the night claiming Kelli, he had danced with Addison quite a bit. Who knew the two of them would've hit it off so well? She was glad they were staying.

She was a little nervous about staying herself.

"We've taken down the point sheets, but I'll say that we've got several people who are very close on points," Graham said, "and we're excited to announce the winners. Meet down here tomorrow at seven-thirty—I know it's early, but we're hoping that you've acclimated to South Carolina time a bit—and we'll announce the winner and have a final goodbye. We'll also have some breakfast items that you can just grab and take with you before you hop on the shuttles to go to the airport."

Merit stood up next to Graham. "Okay, we are done for the night, so feel free to go get some beauty sleep, go out on the town, earn more points, enjoy the game room and theater downstairs, stay up all night, whatever you most want to do. And thank you for spending your Christmas with us. We hope it was as great for you as it was for us."

Kelli jumped to her feet along with everyone else and clapped for Graham and Merit. Then she walked up to them and thanked them personally. They had put so much into planning this for just the twelve of them, and her heart was practically overflowing with gratitude.

Then Parker came up to her and said, "So, how do you want to spend—"

But her phone was buzzing, so she pulled it out of her pocket, looked at the screen, and squealed. "It's my dad! Sorry—I've got to—" He just smiled at her and nodded, and she answered as she raced up to her room.

"Daddy!"

"It's so good to hear your voice, Candy Cane."

"You, too, Dad." It had been too long since she'd last talked with him, especially since it seemed like she'd been vacationing for weeks—or months—already. But she pushed her emotions down and said brightly, "How has your trip been?"

"Not the same without you. I've missed all of our traditions!"

"I've missed them, too," she said, only partially able to keep the emotion from her voice. She brushed a knuckle just below her eye to keep a tear from spilling over. "And I've missed you."

"I've missed you, too. Once we both get back, we need to spend a good amount of time together."

She held the speaking part of the phone away from her mouth as she let out a relieved breath that came out choked with emotion.

"I know that integrating with this new family has taken a lot of my time lately, but I'm anxious to get things going smoothly there so that I can work on integrating you in with them."

He had pushed her away, but he had a plan for bringing

her back in. She was going to get her dad back, and eventually JoAnn and her new stepsisters, too. She wanted to reach through the phone and give him a giant hug.

They were only able to talk for about five minutes before he had to go, but it was a really good five minutes that left her floating on a cloud of happiness. She couldn't wait to tell Parker.

PARKER

PARKER DIDN'T KNOW how long Kelli would be talking to her dad, so he decided to use the time to go to his room and look up things he could do with Kelli during their bonus four days at the resort. The resort had a lot to offer during the winter even when it wasn't over Christmas and New Year's, and they hadn't even begun to check them all out yet. The town of Myrtle Beach had even more things to do, and he couldn't wait for the two of them to do it all.

He barely had time to look, though, before Kelli came into his room, alive with happiness. Her dad hadn't seen her at all over Christmas, and all he could spare her was a five-minute phone call?

"I just had the best phone call with my dad."

"Oh yeah?" He met her partway into his room and wrapped his arms around her waist, then kissed her on her temple. "Tell me about it."

He didn't keep his arms around her, though, because she seemed too full of energy and excitement to stand still. So he sat on his bed as she moved about the room, telling him the story.

"So when my dad first said that they were going away for Christmas, and it was just going to be JoAnn and his new daughters and not me, I felt like I was being pushed away. No—more like left behind. Tossed aside. But I just told myself that it was temporary. It was only coming from JoAnn, not from my dad. Just like how she'd asked her three daughters to be her bridesmaids at the wedding, but didn't ask me. But then my dad asked me to be his best man, so everything was fine in the end."

She seemed so happy and full of life as she was telling him, but he felt stabs of pain in his gut on her behalf. It was all awful, and he was even more impressed that she was as open and happy as she was when she had every right to be closed off and cynical.

"But apparently, I *had* been worried that my dad just didn't want me anymore and would be just as happy if I wasn't around even more than I thought I'd been. Because during our phone call, which was so perfect and amazing, he told me that he missed me that he missed spending Christmas with me, and that he hoped that he'd get integrated with JoAnn's family soon so that he could start integrating me into the family. So it *is* just temporary, and not only am I going to get my dad back, but I'll also be getting a bigger family out of the deal!

"I had no idea how much I believed that would never

happen until he told me it would, and it's like a giant weight has been lifted off me and now I'm flying."

He loved seeing Kelli this happy. Part of him wanted to spin her around in a circle and celebrate with her. But another part of him—a bigger part—was worried that she was just being set up for a fall from a very dangerous, very scary height. That her dad wasn't going to follow through with all that he promised, and she would be back to having a very part-time dad in her life.

And with as excited as she was getting, that fall was going to be crushing and he worried what it would do to her. He just wanted to wrap his arms around her and protect her from such a devastating fall, and to be a soft place to land when she did.

"Kelli," he said, trying to figure out how to tiptoe his way in, "are you sure you want to get so excited yet? I mean, maybe it's better to wait until you see it happening."

She cocked her head to the side and grabbed hold of her elbows with her hands. "You don't think he's telling the truth?"

"No, it's not that. It's just...I don't know. It sounds like JoAnn has a lot of sway over him."

"She does. My dad never would've shut me out of Christmas if it wasn't for her. But I think all of that is because they just got married, and she's trying to look out for her girls. They all still live at home, you know. As my dad said, she just needs time to feel secure in their relationship."

He let out a deep breath and looked out the window before meeting her gaze again. "Maybe just be careful with hoping that things are going to go back to the way they were with you and your dad before he met JoAnn."

"Well, of course, they won't all be the same. He has more people than just me in his life now. But that also doesn't mean things are going to keep going the way they were this Christmas."

"You never know. I mean he did it once." He closed his eyes for a moment, knowing he shouldn't have said that. But he could feel the heat rising in him that her dad had treated her the way that he had, and he really didn't want him to have the chance to do it again. "I just don't want to see you get hurt."

"Parker." She was blinking rapidly now. "I don't know why you aren't being happy about this with me. Everything is going to work out just fine! My dad always has my back. He'll look out for me."

"Except he *didn't* look out for you. Even if this was all JoAnn's choice, your dad didn't say no. He chose a wife and daughters who had only been his family for less than a year, and ignored the daughter he's had for twenty-six years."

Parker wanted to throttle the guy. It was awful that he would make Kelli feel the way that she had, especially when there was so much he could've done so that she wouldn't have had to go through all that. It was so frustrating that he hadn't. While they'd been on the retreat, he'd seen just how badly she'd been hurt by what her dad did, and he wished he could protect her from every bit of pain.

"You don't even know him."

"I just don't get why you are giving him another

chance. What he did was..." *Unforgivable* was how he wanted to end the sentence. But he was her dad, so instead, he just shook his head, looked down at the carpet, and said, "Terrible."

Kelli was quiet long enough that he looked up. She was standing next to his desk, one hand on her hip, and she was looking at him with her eyes narrowed. It was a look he'd never seen on her before.

Finally, she said, "So you think I should just cut him out of my life. The only family I've had for thirteen years. The link to the possibility of becoming more of a family with my new stepmom and my new stepsisters."

"Kelli, I—"

"You don't cut someone out of your life just because they made a mistake." Her voice gave him chills down his back, and he suddenly knew she wasn't talking about her dad anymore.

As soon as he thought about it from her point of view, he realized how what he said could've been taken so wrong. Especially if she was imagining herself as the one making a mistake. But he would never do that to her.

"No, Kelli, I didn't mean it like that. It's just that he's your dad, so family should come first for him." He was scrambling, trying to come up with a way to explain it to her after he had probably done irreparable damage.

His phone, still sitting on the desk where he'd left it, lit up with a message, and both of their eyes were automatically drawn to it. But then Kelli's eyebrows drew together, a confused and hurt look on her face. She stared at it until the screen went dark again, then she looked at him. "You have a job offer?"

Oh, no. He got to the desk in three strides and picked up his phone. The message was from Josh, and although the lock screen didn't show the full message, it showed enough.

> JOSH: I get that this job is your backup plan if things go south at ZentCube (I'm guessing this is about a girl?), but I still plan to work hard to entice you to accept...

He stared at it, and of all the thoughts that could've gone through his head first, Stephanie's list made it to the front. One of the items that annoyed her was that he let his notifications show on his lock screen. Maybe he should've taken that particular critique more seriously.

"I wasn't looking for a job. Josh and I worked together before ZentCube and we became friends. So when his company was looking for a brand manager, he recommended me."

"And you decided that you'd like to stay at ZentCube, but you didn't tell Josh's company no. You're holding on to the job offer, because you're afraid that things won't work out between us, and you don't want to work at the same place as me if they don't."

It sounded so much harsher when she said it, but she'd spelled it out exactly. He couldn't think of a single thing to say that wouldn't make things worse. He pled with his eyes that she would understand that it wasn't as bad as it sounded

—he had just been scared. Scared that he wasn't good enough, and scared that he wouldn't be able to tell when he wasn't, so he wouldn't be able to fix things in time.

"You've got a backup plan so that if I make a mistake, you can easily cut me out of your life."

Her words hit him like a blast, nearly knocking him backward. "That's not it." He reached his hand out halfway to her, but she didn't close the distance with hers. Her hand didn't so much as twitch, so he dropped his arm.

"You are so wrong about my dad. He's a good guy, but you've decided he isn't without even meeting him first."

He ran his hands over his face. There were times when he was able to dismiss Stephanie's whole list as just something created out of her special brand of rudeness. But other times—most of the time—he felt like she'd been spot-on. He could picture her in the room right now, standing with a hand on her hip, an eyebrow cocked, telling him all the ways in which he'd messed up during this one single conversation.

"Parker," Kelli said, her voice softer now. She stepped right up to him and this time she was the one who reached out her hand. He reached forward, almost mechanically, like his mind hadn't decided what to do yet but his body responded anyway, and he let Kelli hold his hand. "I really like you. A lot. A crazy amount. If the two of us are going to work out, you need to trust me more. Be on my side."

He sucked in a deep breath, closing his eyes. The first thing on Stephanie's list was that he hadn't put her as his number one priority. Kelli saying that he hadn't been on her side felt like the same thing. It felt like evidence that

Stephanie had been right about him all along. He wasn't anywhere near good enough for Kelli.

Even though he didn't want to see what his words were going to do to Kelli, he made himself open his eyes and look at her. "I don't think the two of us are going to work out."

She looked at him for a long moment, sadness seeming to fill every inch of her.

"You should take the job," she whispered. Then she dropped his hand and walked out of his room.

Parker spent what was left of the evening in his room, feeling awful about how completely he'd messed things up and replaying all the monumentally stupid things he'd said to Kelli about her dad and the job offer. He had just been awful to her. The look on her face when he'd said that they weren't going to work out was burned into his memory, and it kept playing on repeat. *He* was the one who had caused that expression of devastating grief. Even as much as he loved her, he did that to her.

But he was in the main rooms by seven a.m. the next morning. He was hoping that she would be down a little before the closing ceremony started so he could begin to apologize for being such a jerk. And maybe explain why he had said that he didn't think they would work out. And maybe tell her how wrong it had felt to end things.

Thomas was the only one in the kitchen area that early, so he tried to focus on chatting with him enough to somewhat carry on a conversation when his mind was so far away from it.

A few more people trickled in, most of them going through the items that had been set out to eat for breakfast during the closing ceremony, in the car on the way to the airport, or on the airplane. Still, Kelli didn't come down. She was usually so early to everything. Especially to something like this, where they were going to say goodbyes and announce who got the most points and who won the grand prize.

At seven twenty-five, he stood from the bar stool he'd been sitting on, and he was about to go up to her room to check on her when Graham walked in. As soon as his eyes fell on Parker, a sadness washed over him. He walked straight over to Parker, put his hand on his shoulder, and said, "I'm so sorry to hear about you and Kelli."

"You know?"

Graham nodded. "She told me when she came to me last night and asked if she could fly home today instead of on New Year's Day. *Oh.* She didn't tell you."

Alarm shot through Parker, and he'd taken one step on his way to rush up to her room and try to explain everything and convince her not to leave, but Graham put a hand on his shoulder, stopping him.

"She texted a couple of hours ago, saying that she was taking an Uber to the airport early. She's already gone."

Everything closed in on him, crushing him, as everyone else in the room made their way to the couches in the family room to hear the winner announcement. Everything around him didn't quite seem real, and the world seemed very far away.

"You'll have to excuse me," Parker said as he made his way out the door, and hopefully up to his room before he fell apart.

Nineteen

KELLI

BEFORE KELLI TALKED to Parker last night, if someone had told her that she'd be going home today and that because of her late decision to do so, she wouldn't even get to be on the same flight home with all the new friends she had made, she would've been devastated.

But after everything with Parker, she was glad she didn't know anyone on the plane because she didn't want to talk to a soul. Not even the people on either side of her. She went to the back of the line so she could board last, and the moment she sat down, she put on her headphones—the universal "I don't want to talk" signal.

She didn't even listen to the audiobook she had gotten specifically for the plane ride. She just dusted off her *Sad Songs* playlist and wallowed along with Adele and John Mayer. Parker had been so worried about her getting her hopes up too much that things would work out with her dad. Maybe he was right to worry, and maybe he wasn't. But what Parker really should've been worrying about was her getting her hopes up too much that things would work out with Parker.

Because him ending things with her crushed her more completely than her dad not inviting her to Christmas had, which she hadn't even thought was possible.

He had just been so harsh about her dad. Way more than he needed to be. It was good that she got to witness the side of him that saw things as black and white, right or wrong, without considering everything. She could never be with someone where she had to worry if he was going to judge her just as harshly for a mistake she made. She should be happy she discovered this side of him early. She should be thrilled that he broke things off before she got invested even more.

So why wasn't she?

Probably because she had discovered a lot of other sides of him, too. As the plane flew from the east coast toward the west, she couldn't stop thinking about how much she enjoyed spending time with him, how easy it was to talk with him, how quick he was to laugh or tell a joke, and how great it was that she could get him to go do fun things at the spur of the moment.

And how quick he was to help people. When they had spent hours on the cold bench on Christmas Eve, she talked about what she wanted to do to get ZentCube employees to help at the soup kitchen in Denver. Not only had he been encouraging, but he said he'd be the first to sign up.

And he was so cute with the kids at the Christmas Village. And seeing the way he held Graham's baby had made her heart melt into a pile of goo. She wanted to have kids someday, and she wanted their dad to look at them exactly the way Parker had looked at baby Hope.

And he'd been so kind and inclusive at the Tinsel and Tidings Ball. She was so impressed at how he'd looked out for her. He was always looking out for her, more than just at the ball.

She closed her eyes and let the memory of how it had felt to have his strong arms around her when she was scared. His arms made her feel safe and protected like there wasn't a fear in the world that he couldn't quell. Even the thought of it made warmth spread throughout her body, bringing with it the feeling of peace she had when they'd been so close.

That morphed into the memory of how it had felt with his arms cradling her when she was sad. The way he listened and comforted her and made her feel that no matter how bad things got, everything would be okay. She wished those arms were around her now, comforting her and telling her everything would be okay.

Right now, she desperately wanted to see again the way a smile spread across his face whenever she walked into the room, showing that dimple on his cheek.

Then another memory hit her. The very first day, when Merit had introduced Elise, she had wished and hoped and craved to one day have a man look at her the same way Merit looked at Elise. The realization that she had gotten her wish —that the way Parker looked at her was exactly like that— was difficult to bear. She had wanted so badly for things to work out between them.

As she sat in her seat, headphones on and eyes closed, silent tears rolled down her face and fell into her lap. Maybe she would never be able to hold on to a love like that. Maybe the memory of it was all she would ever have.

The plane touched down at Denver International and it hit her that she had been so wrapped up in thoughts of Parker that she hadn't even thought about where she was long enough to be apprehensive about the takeoff or landing.

She wiped the last few tears from her cheeks, removed her headphones, wrapped them up, and placed them into the side pocket of her bag.

"Are you okay?"

Kelli looked at the person in the aisle seat for the first time—a man in his thirties who looked very uncomfortable asking, yet also very concerned—and she nodded. Although she could still feel his concerned gaze on her, he thankfully didn't ask any more questions.

As she got off the plane, walked down to baggage claim, got her suitcase, got on the shuttle to the car lot, then got in her car and drove home on snow-lined streets, she thought about the guys she had dated before. She had felt a connection with a few of them. She had with James, too, actually, although that connection came very slowly.

She had never felt it as strongly, though, as she had with Parker during their week that felt like two months. Maybe it had been longer than that. Maybe she had felt it from the other side of the second floor of the marketing building at ZentCube ever since he started working there just over two and a half years ago. Maybe that was why their pranks had continued over such a long period when they hardly saw each other through their normal work tasks.

She just hadn't known how strong that connection would grow to be until they both boarded a plane headed to the other side of the country.

When she finally pulled into the parking lot in front of her apartment, right next to a monstrous pile of snow left by the snow plow, she grabbed her suitcases out of her car and headed up to her place. As soon as she opened the door, two warring emotions hit her. Comfort and relief at finally being home again after a long vacation, and a sudden empty loneliness, like a home after everything is packed up in a moving truck.

Normally, she wouldn't do anything before unpacking her suitcase and getting everything perfectly in its spot. But today, she just left them next to the front door, trudged to her bedroom, climbed into bed, and pulled the covers over her head.

Twenty

PARKER

Parker missed the announcement of the winner at the closing ceremony.

He missed saying goodbye to Graham, Tessa, baby Hope, and the eight other ZentCube Employees who were flying home.

He missed lunch.

He missed Kelli.

It was late afternoon before he finally managed to drag himself out of his room and down to the beach. Not to run—he didn't have the energy to do that. Instead, he just walked along the same section of beach that he and Kelli had walked so long ago. Although it hadn't actually been that long ago. Somehow, it already felt like she had been a part of his life always. He was so grateful that Stephanie had broken off their engagement or he would've never gotten this second chance with Kelli.

He just wished he hadn't blown that chance.

He should've been working on the list that Stephanie had given him from the moment she'd put it in his hands. Right at the very top of her list had been *Not putting me as the #1 thing in your life.* He hadn't understood at the time why she had that on the list at all because he thought he *had* been putting her first.

But now he got it. Now that he realized he did the same thing to Kelli. If she had been the number one thing in his life, then his issues about her dad wouldn't have taken the driver's seat. He would've done everything possible to keep her radiating that happiness that had seemed too big to contain when she'd first come into his room to tell him about her dad.

In looking back with the benefit—or the curse—of hindsight, he could see so very clearly how much damage he had inflicted when he'd said the things he had.

On the woman he loved.

He couldn't walk any further, so he just sat on a nearby bench, staring out at the ocean as wave after wave came onto the shore. The entire sky was filled with gray clouds that seemed to pull the color from the ocean, and the cool breeze bit into his skin.

He thought back to the carriage ride and how it felt to have her snuggled up into him, her head on his shoulder, her breath on his neck, his arms wrapped around her. He thought about sitting next to her on the bench in the center of The Royal Palm's grounds in the middle of the night, the two of them huddled together for warmth, spending hours sharing their hopes, their fears, their pasts, and their dreams.

He would give anything to have her sitting next to him on this bench right now.

Or to see the way she quirked one eyebrow when she was amused or pulled on the corner of her bottom lip with her teeth when she was concentrating. Or to watch the way she led with her heart on every decision. The way she looked out for others. The way she let herself feel everything deeply, yet never dwelled on the shortcomings of others. The way she immediately saw the best in others, whether it was her first time meeting them or someone she had known her entire life.

No matter how many times she got knocked down, she stood back up. Even at times when most people would've stayed down for a while.

And then his breathing hitched when he thought about the moment he'd looked across the Christmas Village and had seen her holding baby Hope. He had known his whole life that he wanted to be a dad and have kids, but he'd never actually been able to picture anyone he dated as being the future mother of his children until that moment.

She was soft and compassionate, organized and playful, trusting and non-judgmental. She was terrified of spiders and complete darkness, yet she showed incredible inner strength and resilience time and time again. She was someone not to be underestimated. She was an enigma that he wanted to spend his life figuring out.

Darren had said he thought Parker was ready to open his heart again. And the surprising thing was, Darren had been right. There was one missing piece still, though. Parker hadn't already become the man who was worthy of her.

KELLI

A KNOCK SOUNDED on Kelli's front door, but she was too sick to get out of bed to go answer it.

Then she heard "I'm using my old key and coming in" loudly enough that she was pretty sure any neighbors who were home heard Valeria's voice, too. A moment later, her friend walked into her room.

"How are you feeling?" Val asked while setting down various bags and putting things on her nightstand.

Kelli paused the Hallmark Christmas movie she'd been watching. "About as awful as I look." And then a coughing fit hit, and she grabbed a tissue to cover her mouth, her brain feeling like it was getting beat up inside her head with every cough.

"Well, I guess getting the world's biggest cold is one way to distract yourself from the heartbreak."

Kelli shrugged and dropped the crumpled tissue on her floor with the others. It hurt her soul to have them all just

183

making a mess of her floor, but she had been too exhausted to get out of bed and move her trash container closer. "If I'm going to feel awful, I might as well deal with them both at the same time."

This was the worst cold she had gotten in a whole lot of years. On second thought, she probably wouldn't have chosen to double it up with anything.

Valeria placed the back of her hand on Kelli's forehead. "No fever still. That's good because I brought soup." She pulled from a bag two containers of soup, a stack of napkins, and two spoons. She glanced once at the Hallmark movie-watching blanket that was spread across Kelli, but instead of bringing it up, she asked, "Have you heard back from Liz yet?"

Kelli was grateful Valeria wasn't bringing up Parker. Everything was still too bright and painful and fresh. Liz, she could talk about. Liz, she could even smile about. "I did. She hadn't already gone in to look at the ad campaign yet, but she looked and told me not to stress out, that these things happen. It's all part of the game. You win some and you lose some, and I have a track record for winning more than I lose, so it's all good."

Valeria grinned as she carried the soup to the other side of Kelli's bed and put it on the nightstand furthest away, then climbed onto the bed and sat down next to her. "I told you it would all be fine. Now push play." She grabbed both containers of soup and handed one to Kelli.

They watched and ate soup, commenting only on the movie, for several long minutes before Valeria said,

"Remember when Rhett and I broke up and I barely got off the couch for three days?"

"I think I've got your look beat. But yeah—you were a mess."

"Yet, that didn't stop you from loving me, and it didn't make you kick me out of BFF status."

"Of course not!"

"And I still love you, too. Your name is practically tattooed as my BFF."

Kelli grinned at her, unsure why her friend was getting all sentimental on her but liking it all the same.

"Since I was your roommate for two years, I've seen you be imperfect plenty of times."

Kelli looked back at her, wary. Whatever turn Valeria was taking this conversation on, she no longer liked it.

"I mean, it wasn't often. But you think your less-than-perfect moments only happen when Parker's around? What about that time you decided to make scones for the first time and thought the oil needed to come to a boil to show that it was ready? I'm surprised you didn't burn the kitchen down when you dropped that first one in. And I'm pretty sure that we could find something in the apartment that still carries the stench of The Smoke that Permeated Everything."

Heat flamed to Kelli's face just remembering it. Now it seemed so stupid that she ever thought the oil was supposed to boil, yet at the time, it had made perfect sense. It still surprised her how quickly that scone flash-burned to black.

"And the time you couldn't sleep during the night so you got up and rearranged all the furniture in the living room but didn't tell me. So when I woke up and shuffled toward the kitchen, groggy and still half asleep, I stumbled into the corner of the armchair and fell and nearly sprained my wrist."

Maybe she did have a fever because her face was on fire. "Thanks, Val. I'd been doing a pretty good job of repressing those things."

Valeria put her soup container on the nightstand and turned to face her, sitting with her legs crossed. "The point is, I still love you. In fact, those things made me love you more because I got to see the real you. I like when you're imperfect."

Kelli smiled. And might have gotten a little teary. But that might have just been the watery eyes from her cold. "That's why you're the best, Valeria."

"It's not just me." Valeria huffed out a breath, her eyes aimed at the ceiling, thinking, like she was frustrated that she wasn't getting her point across and trying to figure out how. "Okay, do you know what? I'm just going to come right out and say it." She took a deep breath. "Your mom didn't leave because you're imperfect. She did because *she* is imperfect."

Kelli gasped as the blow of talking about her mom hit her.

"Your dad didn't keep from inviting you to join him, his wife, and his new stepdaughters for Christmas because *you're* imperfect. They did because *they* are imperfect. We all are. Every single one of us. That's what makes us human and beautiful and yes, even *lovable*."

Tears were falling in earnest now. Kelli set her soup on her nightstand.

Then Valeria whispered, "And Parker isn't going to stop loving you because you're imperfect or because you make a mistake. And he isn't going to stop loving you just because *he's* imperfect, too."

Kelli grabbed a tissue and started wiping at her eyes. "I want to believe you, Val. I do. And I totally believe in the concept. About other people. I'm just... not sure that I believe it deep down. About me."

"All right. I'm going to list off all the embarrassing things that have happened around Parker, just on this trip alone. Now, you might have to help me if I don't remember all of the ones you told me. But in my defense, the list is *long*."

Kelli laughed through her tears and swatted her friend with the back of her hand. Then she blew her nose.

"The water landing in your lap on the plane, making it look like you didn't make it to the bathroom in time. Drooling all over him when you accidentally fell asleep on him. Taking your poor row neighbor's luggage, flinging a mushroom into his water, tripping with the cookies while caroling, singing the wrong verse while caroling, twisting your ankle at dinner—"

"Okay, stop! You don't need to name them all—I think we've established that lots of embarrassing things happened." Her face was flaming hot all over again.

"But he still kept falling for you, through it all."

Kelli closed her eyes. He had. No matter how many

embarrassing things happened, he still kept wanting to be with her. Right up until the end, when he ended things with no real explanation. "Val?" she said, her voice quivering. "He was so upset about my dad."

"Kelli." Valeria paused until Kelli met her eyes. "It's because he's in love with you and doesn't want anyone to hurt you."

She studied her friend's eyes, trying to figure out if what she was saying felt true. "I don't know if he's in love with me. He broke up with me, Val. That's not what 'in love' people do."

"Sometimes 'in love' people get a little scared."

Kelli flinched back in surprise. "Why? That makes no sense."

"When Rhett and I broke up, part of the reason was because he was scared and a little insecure. I didn't find out that part until after we got married and he told me." Valeria shrugged. "Maybe Parker worries that he's not good enough."

Kelli shook her head. "He's perfect. That can't be it."

Valeria chuckled. "How much do you want to bet that he feels the same way about you?"

Kelli's head was pounding and her sinuses ached, so it was a little more difficult to think, leaving her feeling slightly bewildered. "We broke up, Val. *He* broke up. Do you really think there could still be a chance for us?"

Valeria got off the bed and walked back around to Kelli's side. "Sweetie, I think you're two amazing people who are perfect for each other, and soon you'll both figure that out."

Kelli studied her friend for a long moment and then grabbed a tissue just in time to block a gigantic sneeze. "So what do I do?" Her nose was stuffier from the sneeze and the words didn't come out quite right.

"Get better. Right now, getting better is your only job."

Valeria crouched by the sacks she had set on the floor. "Now, I don't know if you've noticed the passage of time as you've been dwelling here in your cave of broken hearts and mammoth colds, but it's officially New Year's Eve, and I," she said, pulling items out of her bags, "brought decorations!"

PARKER

WHEN PARKER finally pulled himself out of bed, he went downstairs to the mansion's kitchen to try to find something for breakfast. He didn't want to leave the place to go find food—there was so much festiveness going on at the resort, and he felt anything but festive.

Addison was sitting at the island counter on a barstool, reading on her phone and eating an apple. She glanced up as he walked in. "Hey, Parker."

"Morning."

She sat her phone down. "Parker. It's been three days, and you're still looking like you belong in a movie about an apocalypse."

He let out a single huff of a humorless laugh. "It's not a movie." He turned his back to her, looking on the rear counter for any more fruit.

"I might have been a little jealous of Kelli when we first got here."

Parker turned around at the mention of Kelli's name.

She shrugged. "But I've gotten to know her, and the truth is, she's a pretty cool person."

"I know."

"And she deserves a good guy."

He was very painfully aware of that. "I know."

"And it was obvious from day one that you're a good guy, Parker."

He studied Addison for a moment. The comment seemed genuine, but she hadn't known him well enough to know all of his shortcomings. Instead of responding, he opened the fridge.

"Read this before you look for food. It was here on the counter when I came down."

She tossed a piece of paper in his direction, and he caught it before it drifted off the edge of the counter. It was a note from Merit, asking Parker to meet him at the Green Olive in the clubhouse at nine for breakfast. He glanced down at his watch—it was already eight-forty. He probably shouldn't have chosen this as the one day to sleep in.

He thanked Addison, hurried upstairs to shower and change, and then jogged over to the clubhouse, trying to ignore all the work going on to get the place set up for the New Year's celebration going on tonight. The dinner, live music, and dance that was going to be outside under the stars, with fireworks and a toast to the new year, along with kissing at midnight. The event that he was supposed to attend with Kelli.

Darren, Adam, and several other friends had texted or

called since the morning Kelli flew back home. He hadn't responded to any of them—he just hadn't been ready to talk. Yet Merit was sure to bring everything up.

He glanced at his watch as he stepped into the lobby. It was a few minutes after nine. The place still had the Christmas tree and most of the Christmas decorations that had been there when he came with Kelli, but some had been switched out for gold, silver, and black New Year's decorations, and somehow, all of it looked right together.

The hostess directed Parker to a table where Merit sat, just as the waiter was setting down several plates of food.

Merit looked at Parker and said, "Oh, good, you made it," before thanking the waiter. "I'm glad you got my note. I ordered food already. I hope that's okay."

"Of course."

An empty plate sat in front of each of them, and all the plates with food were in the middle of the table, filled with eggs, bacon, pancakes, hash browns, fruit, and toast.

"I didn't know what you'd like, so I got a little of everything. Dish up."

As they put food on their plates and started eating, Merit asked him questions about the retreat. It felt mostly like small talk, but he figured the guy probably wanted to know if things needed to be tweaked for their next retreat. So he pushed his feelings of sadness and remorse aside, focused on the conversation, and answered everything honestly and openly. It was better to talk about this stuff, anyway. He could convince himself that they were just two guys chatting about a work thing without a care in the world.

He was caught completely off guard when Merit asked, "So have you decided whether or not to take that other job?"

He had *almost* forgotten that he had told Merit about the job offer. Not that he couldn't remember telling him—it was just that neither Merit nor Graham had brought it up a single time on the retreat, so he just hadn't thought about it. He nodded. "I turned it down. I'm going to stay at ZentCube."

A smile spread across Merit's face. "We're glad you're staying. You're good at what you do, and we're fortunate to have you." Merit looked down at his plate for a moment, a small smile on his lips, before he looked back at Parker. "Although I'm sure it wasn't just a matter of us convincing you that this was a good company to stay with. I'd bet that Kelli had more to do with your decision than we did."

"You convinced me," he reassured Merit. "This is a great company."

Merit raised an eyebrow in a look that told him that he didn't like it when people just said what they thought he wanted to hear. He liked it when they told it straight. Parker knew enough about Merit to know that already; his response had been less about protecting Merit's feelings and more about protecting his own.

"Okay, she did have a lot to do with the decision. If I can someday be good enough for her, then I want to see her while I'm at work, too. If I can't, then I deserve to be reminded daily of what I lost."

"Ouch." Merit flinched, like that pain hit him, too. "Do you love her?"

Parker's nod came quickly. "More than I ever thought I could love another person. She's funny and thoughtful and has the most incredible inner strength. Just being around her makes me want to be a better man."

"So what happened?"

Parker exhaled slowly, trying to figure out how to tell Merit. He was embarrassed and didn't want to admit how foolish he'd been, but he realized that not responding to any of his friends who had reached out hadn't been working out so great for him, either. He just really needed to talk it out.

"If you would've asked me what Kelli's biggest fear was before we came on this trip, I would've guessed spiders. I've realized that it's a fear of people walking out of her life. But I didn't understand that until I said some stupid things that made her believe that she needs to fear that with me."

"Does she?"

"No!" Parker swallowed hard. "Except I kind of did when I ended things with her. I didn't even want things to end."

Merit picked up his glass of orange juice and swirled it around for a moment before he drank the last of it and set the glass back down. He met Parker's eyes. "Graham and I are both surprised that you haven't come to me asking if you can get your flight changed to an earlier time. He's been texting several times a day, asking if you've come to talk to me yet. It's New Year's Eve already—why are you still here and not back in Denver, trying to convince her that she doesn't need to fear that with you?"

"Because I want her to be with someone good enough

for her." Parker swallowed down a lump in his throat. "And I don't think I am."

"Do you want to be?"

"Of course I do."

Merit's phone lit up with a text, and he typed a response before continuing. "I've noticed that Kelli is a bit of a perfectionist."

Parker chuckled. "You could say that. Which is crazy, because she's perfect even when she's not trying to be."

Merit studied him for long enough that it made him flinch. This wasn't his boss studying him—this was the CEO, the co-founder, and the co-owner of the huge company Parker worked for. This was by far more intense than any time Adam's focus was on him. It made him feel exposed, as if Merit could see anything about him that he wanted to.

"Have you ever noticed that you're a bit of a perfectionist, too?"

Parker rubbed his forehead, frowning. He hadn't ever thought that of himself.

"Parker, if there's anything I've learned by falling in love with Elise, it's that Kelli doesn't need you to be perfect. *Nobody* needs to be perfect. It's only ever about recognizing your shortcomings and working to overcome them. You have your own incredible strength of character. Graham and I wouldn't have brought you on this trip otherwise. Every amazing person I've ever met has gotten there by continually working to become better. Never because they're working to become perfect, only that they're working to be better today than they were yesterday.

"So work to be better. Make it a habit to apologize sincerely when you're wrong. And let her know how you feel about her already."

Parker shook his head. "I don't know." All of that made sense logically. And he could see it working. But what about the long term? "I'm just... not good at being able to tell when things start to go wrong."

"This ex-fiancée of yours—from what you told me, you were blindsided when she gave you this list, right?"

"Very much so."

"Okay. Were you blindsided when things went wrong with Kelli?"

"Yeah."

His answer had come quickly, but Merit was still looking at him like he was waiting for him to think it through, so he did. Things had been going well. But he'd had his own fears he'd been working through, and looking back, he could easily see when those things were impacting things with Kelli, even before their disastrous conversation.

And from what he knew about Kelli's mom leaving and her dad's new family, she had plenty of fears she was working through, too. He knew all of that and knew it could be an issue.

And then he thought about the conversation in his room about her dad. He had looked at her face several times during that conversation and saw what it was doing to her.

Yet he still kept talking, still kept saying things about her dad.

Had he even meant everything that he had said? Had he forgotten that she was much more important than any negative opinions he had of her dad? Or had he simply been allowing his fears to take over, and subconsciously sabotaged everything with a single, terrible, hurtful conversation? He wasn't sure, and the weight of what he'd done hit him anew.

He shook his head. "I wasn't blindsided."

Merit nodded, and then he picked up his phone, touching several things while he spoke. "Graham wanted in on this conversation. And since he's Graham, he sent his contribution in the form of a slideshow."

Parker chuckled as Merit turned his phone toward him. Graham must've had the slides set to a timer because each one switched to the next on its own. The first slide was of the twelve of them who had come on the retreat—the same bobble-headed images from the slideshow Graham had presented on the first day—standing in front of the limos, holding their luggage, with sounds of cheering.

Most of them had a bag and a suitcase, but Parker seemed to have the most luggage of them all. He had the bag and suitcase but also wore a huge backpack like the kind hikers take when they want to stay overnight somewhere and they have to pack in all of their bedding, shelter, clothing, food, and cooking supplies. It was big enough that it even rose higher than his head.

Then it switched to the second slide, and a slow, instrumental song played through Merit's phone's speakers as bobble-headed Parker and bobble-headed Kelli danced, which wasn't easy with their bodies that were so much smaller than their heads. The luggage was gone, but Parker was still wearing the giant backpack.

The next slide came with the sound of forks clinking on plates, and bobble-headed Kelli was smiling at bobble-headed Parker as they both served food at the soup kitchen. The backpack was still on Parker's back.

As the next slide came on the screen, the song that Merit and Graham had sung to wake them up Christmas morning —*We Wish You a Merry Christmas*—played, as all seventeen of them sat around a Christmas tree, including baby Hope in Tessa's arms. Parker was holding a Christmas present out to Kelli and, of course, he was still wearing the backpack.

The next slide was split into two. On the left was an outline of the state of Colorado, with a bobble-headed crying Kelli in the middle of it; on the right was South Carolina with a bobble-headed crying Parker, still wearing the backpack. He couldn't say he'd cried, but the image still captured how brokenhearted he felt.

The next slide was of a plane on a runway. An animated Parker threw off the backpack and then ran with his suitcase to the plane. Then it switched to bobble-headed Parker and bobble-headed Kelli kissing, a love song playing in the background.

The visuals, fun and cartoony as they were, hit him hard. But at the same time, they filled him with hope.

Merit smiled, shaking his head, as he closed out of the

slideshow. "Graham is nothing if not theatrical in his slideshows. I think the point he got across without using a single word was that it's easy to project the baggage from a past relationship onto the next, Parker. We've all done it. Just remember that Kelli and your ex aren't the same. *You* aren't even the same. So don't let your past ruin something pretty great in your future."

Parker swallowed, letting Merit's words and Graham's pictures sink in. "I can see why ZentCube is so successful. You're pretty wise."

Merit laughed. "I wouldn't go that far. It wasn't that long ago that I made my own monumental mistakes when it came to falling in love with an incredible woman, and I was grateful to have someone step in and help me get past it." He reached into the pocket of his jacket, pulled out a folded piece of paper, and then slid it across the table. "The earliest flight I could get you leaves this afternoon. A car will be by to pick you up at two."

"Thank you, Merit." He couldn't express how grateful he was, but he hoped Merit could see it on his face. He seemed to be good at that.

He picked up the paper without opening it, his mind racing to figure out what he should do once he landed in Denver.

Twenty-Three

KELLI

A KNOCK SOUNDED at Kelli's door. She glanced at her clock—it was after eleven p.m.—then shook her head. She thought she'd fully convinced Valeria that she was just fine and didn't need her babysitting all night and that she should go celebrate New Year's Eve with Rhett.

Before the trip to the Royal Palm Resort, before the plan to extend the trip over New Year's, before everything with Parker happened, and before this cold decided to take up residence in her body, she had planned to go to the same party and had been excited about it. The place was even going to have a light show in the ballroom as they counted down to midnight, and as much as she didn't want to be alone tonight, she didn't want Valeria to miss it even more.

She cleared her throat the best she could in its current state and called out, "Come in! And you better be coming back only because you forgot something!"

She heard the key turn in the lock, but she started

coughing because yelling that loud had been too much for her poor, scratchy throat. The coughing made her head pound and angered her sinuses. She was just blowing her stuffy nose when Parker appeared in her bedroom doorway.

"Parker!"

She stared at him with her mouth open, wondering if she was really seeing him standing in her doorway, holding bags, snow in his hair and on his shoulders, the light she'd left on in her living room backlighting him and making him look like an angel. Was she seeing things?

"What are you doing here? Aren't you in Myrtle Beach? You don't even know where I live! And how did you get into my house?" More and more questions filled her mind, but they were coming too fast to get any of them out of her mouth.

He took one tentative step into her room. "I just got back an hour ago. I emailed Valeria to see if she knew where I could find you. She had me meet her at some party and gave me your key. She told me you were sick and that I should come tonight and let myself in so you didn't have to get out of bed." His eyes quickly scanned the room and then fell back on her. "Is it okay that I'm here?"

Kelli gave him a slow nod, and then closed her eyes, thinking about how much she wanted to strangle her best friend. Just because Valeria thought Kelli needed to realize that she didn't have to be perfect didn't mean that she wanted Parker to see her like this. She had managed to shower last night, but hadn't even blow-dried her hair; she had just let it do whatever it wanted to do, and then she'd pulled it into a crazy bun on top of her head.

She hadn't so much as put on moisturizer, let alone the makeup she always put on before ever leaving the house. She was sure her nose was red and dry, especially from blowing it right before Parker appeared in her doorway. And her eyes were probably giant bags from crying earlier. Likely bloodshot, too, based on how itchy they had been and how terribly she'd been sleeping.

And she was wearing flannel pajamas, in bed, and her room looked like a bomb went off in a tissue factory. This was not the way she had wanted to see Parker again, especially after so many embarrassing things had happened in his presence.

But he was there. When he was supposed to be celebrating New Year's Eve on the beach. What did that mean? Her brain was feeling too sick to be able to figure out things like that. She needed Valeria there to translate.

"Can I come in?"

She nodded and motioned to a reading chair she had on the other side of her nightstand. He put his bags down and then sat, but he scooted the chair so that he was facing her. Her overhead light wasn't on, just her two lamps, but it was plenty to see his face in their soft glow.

So many emotions were battling it out inside her, right alongside her massive cold. A thrill had gone through her at seeing him, and it was coursing through her even more madly now that he was so close and his eyes were on hers. There was also an overwhelming sadness that he had ended things. Panic and embarrassment were fighting for dominance, too, and making her wish she'd never said he could come into the room to see her like this. And there was curiosity as to why he had come. That one seemed to be winning.

"I'm sorry you're so sick." He reached a hand forward like he was going to brush his knuckles down her temples. He pulled his hand back, seeming unsure, but her skin was still on high alert and practically tingling with anticipation of his touch. "When did it hit?"

"Not long after I got back. Hopefully, I didn't give it to you before I knew I had it."

The awkwardness was crowding in the room, causing uncomfortable silences and uncertainty. Like they both were bursting with so much to say, but didn't know how to say it. Like they didn't remember how to be around each other since they had officially broken up.

"How's everything with your dad?"

"Good. Some crazy weather delayed his flight, so he doesn't get home until tomorrow afternoon now, but we're going to spend the evening together." Just like her dad had promised. He might not make choices that she agreed with, especially when it came to JoAnn, but he didn't lie. He didn't make promises he couldn't keep. She wished that Parker understood that about him.

Before it had a chance to turn into another awkward silence, she hurried to ask him a question. "When do you start working at your friend's company?" She didn't want to hear the answer. She didn't want to face the idea of him not being at ZentCube daily to become a reality. But she had to know how much time she had left. Hopefully, his answer wouldn't be the day they were supposed to go back to work after the holiday break.

What she wanted to do was ask him to explain why he ended things. She wanted to tell him that she was working on her fears and that she loved him and wanted him to be with her through it. And if he had fears, that she wanted to be with him as he worked through his. She wanted to keep trying to make it through whatever they faced together. That she loved him for who he was.

But she couldn't think straight. Not with this cold and not with him unexpectedly there, sitting so near. She grabbed a tissue and rubbed at her nose. She'd asked Valeria what she needed to do, and all her friend had said was for her to get better. Since she hadn't done that step yet, she hadn't worked out what came next.

Parker moved to the front of his seat, barely sitting on it, leaning forward with his arms resting on his knees. "Kelli, I was wrong. About so many things—most of which I hadn't even realized at the time. I was wrong to say all the things I did about your dad. You were right. I didn't know him well enough to say what I did.

"But I did know you well enough to know that I shouldn't have doubted you. I shouldn't have worried that you would get hurt. I should've just been there for you."

Her breath hitched and a warmth spread through her as his earnest words wrapped around her. He stood and moved to the edge of her bed, sitting by her knees, like he was too far away and needed to get closer, and she could barely breathe.

"Kelli, I am so sorry. I know that what I said hurt you, and I don't ever want to hurt you again. I want to be the one to protect you from anything that could ever harm you. I am every bit as scared that I'm not nearly good enough for you as I was back in my room at The Royal Palm. I wish I was already the kind of man you deserve. All I can do is promise you that I'll never stop trying to be."

Maybe it was the cold, but she was so confused. She reached a hand up and touched his face. "But you're perfect already."

He smiled and leaned into her hand. "I think that's the cold talking."

She laughed. "You were perfect before I got sick."

He just looked at her in dazed awe, like he thought she might be perfect, too, instead of looking like death came by for a visit. "And I think you're amazing every second of every day."

"Even if I cover your work area with cats? Or steal the conference room?"

A smile spread across Parker's face, showing his dimple. "Even then."

He reached for her hands, but she jerked hers back. "Wait!" She was sick, and she didn't want Parker to risk getting what she had. She grabbed the bottle of hand sanitizer from her nightstand and rubbed a generous amount on her hands, then waved them back and forth so they'd dry.

Then she reached toward him and, chuckling, he took

her hands in his. "I love you, Kelli. Please tell me that you'll give me another chance."

I love you. He'd said, *"I love you."* The emotion swelled up in her so much that she could barely keep the tickle it had caused in her throat from turning into a cough.

"Well," she said, "I think that's a distinct possibility because it just so happens that I am madly in love with you, too."

The look of happiness on Parker's face made her feel warm down to her toes and made her wish that she had mistletoe hanging right above her bed. And that she wasn't sick, obviously. She also wanted to get up and pretend that they were at The Royal Palm Resort like they had planned, dancing the night away—this time as an actual dating couple. Her first dance with him had been so amazing that she wanted to spend every chance she could get for the rest of her life dancing with him.

Instead, she motioned to the bags. "What did you bring?"

Parker smiled like she imagined he did when he was fifteen and his little brother realized that Santa had come, and he pulled the bags toward him. From one, he pulled out a mini Christmas tree and set it on her nightstand. She scooted closer to look at the ornaments under the glow of her lamp.

"I found a shop on the boardwalk that had a bunch of unique ornaments."

There was an airplane, a person sleeping, a couple danc-ing, a cooked turkey, a lamppost with Christmas lights wrapped around it, a train, reindeer antlers, a gingerbread house, a little bottle with sand and seashells inside, a horse and carriage, a group Christmas caroling, a cat, and even a mushroom. Seeing all of them made her want to laugh and sigh and cry happy tears and snuggle up in his arms.

"This is amazing, Parker. I've—" She was speechless. Words couldn't express all that she was feeling.

He reached down into the sack and pulled out a present wrapped in beautiful red and gold paper with a tag that read *Kelli* and placed it under the tree. "This one isn't actually from me, but you once accused me of practically gift-wrapping it and putting it under the tree with your name on it, so it felt appropriate to do just that."

She gasped and stared at him for one heartbeat before grabbing the present and opening it. A plain box was inside, and she lifted off the lid to see a single piece of paper that looked like a certificate and read, *THE GRAND PRIZE WINNER OF OUR CHRISTMAS CONTEST IS KELLI ELLIS! AND, AS THE WINNER, IS HEREBY AWARDED THREE EXTRA VACATION DAYS, PARKING SPACE C7 FOR A FULL YEAR, AND LUNCH FOR HER TEAM EVERY WEEK FOR A YEAR.* It was signed by Merit Casselman and Graham McNeil.

Her eyes flew to Parker. "I won?"

He grinned. "Of course. No one could come close to doing all you did."

She leaned back against her headboard. "So I get you *and* parking spot C7, all on the same day."

He leaned forward and gave her the sweetest kiss on the

forehead. "And you get my grandma's famous 'Cold Begone.'" She gave him a questioning look, and he bent down and picked up one of the bags he brought. "It's a warm drink with honey, lemon, apple cider vinegar, cayenne, and ginger. Not only will it speed up your recovery time, but it'll make your throat feel better practically instantly."

"No offense, but that sounds pretty gross."

He smiled big again, showing off those dimples. "I know, but it isn't. Trust me. I'll even drink a cup with you." Then he walked out of the room, and she could hear him doing things in the kitchen. He hadn't even brought her the warm drink yet, and already her chest felt warm, just knowing that she and Parker were going to work out.

He came back a few minutes later, holding two mugs, still steaming, and she scooted over in her bed. He handed her one mug and then sat beside her, putting an arm around her shoulder. She snuggled into him, just like she had on the carriage ride, laying her head on his shoulder and cradling the mug in her hands.

She smelled the drink—it didn't *smell* awful. But still, she waited until he took a drink and watched his face for any signs of it being awful. When she saw none, she blew on hers.

But before she took a sip, he said, "Wait. Hang on." He put the mug on her nightstand, then pulled out his phone and opened the browser, then set it between them and picked up his mug again. It was the official New Year countdown, and it only had about thirty seconds before the year would end and a fresh new one, full of possibilities, would rush in. When only ten seconds were left, they counted down together.

Right as the New Year started, they clinked their mugs of Cold Begone together and each took a sip. It wasn't exactly sparkling champagne, but to her surprise, it actually tasted good and made her aching throat rejoice.

Parker kissed her temple, his warm, soft lips pressing into her skin so gently and so sweetly that it made her sigh. "Happy New Year, Kelli," he whispered, and she knew it would be.

Epilogue

Parker felt like he'd waited his entire life for this day. Guests were filing in and taking their seats on both sides of the aisle, his bride-to-be was in the bride's room with his mom and Valeria, he was surrounded by loved ones, and his tux fit perfectly. The excitement bubbling up in him to see Kelli walking down the aisle was too much to contain, so he went from person to person, chatting, hoping that would use some of the energy.

His dad put his hand on his shoulder to get his attention. "We're going to go say hello to the Garlands." Parker nodded and smiled as his dad and Ethan, who was now as tall as he was, headed over to greet their family friends just as Kelli's dad, Richard, stepped over to him.

"With as many last-minute hiccups as we've had, it looks like this is coming together."

"It is." Parker looked around the venue that was filled with white Christmas trees, the silver and gold lights on them casting a warm glow through the room, and he definitely felt some Christmas magic at work. He had always wanted to get married at Christmastime, and since that was when he and Kelli had fallen in love, it felt exactly right.

He turned to his soon-to-be father-in-law. "Thanks again for agreeing to be my best man. It means a lot to both of us."

Richard nodded. "Thank you for asking me. It means a lot to me as well."

He hugged the man. The two of them had come a long way in the past year. Although Parker still thought Kelli's dad had made a terrible mistake by not celebrating last Christmas with his daughter, he was hardly the only one making mistakes. Parker had been so worried that Kelli had been setting herself up to get hurt again, but he knew now how much he should trust her judgment on matters like that. Giving people the benefit of the doubt the way she did had made his life richer as well.

Besides, if Richard hadn't left Kelli alone last Christmas, the two of them might not have ever gotten past their fears enough to even go out on a second date. So maybe he should've been thanking the man all along.

As Richard went off toward JoAnn, Parker found himself pulled toward the other three men in tuxes: Valeria's husband, Rhett, who had become his best friend over the past year, and Merit and Graham. He shook their hands and thanked them for being part of the wedding party.

Merit was wearing a wedding ring now, which made Parker smile. Baby Hope was now a toddler who was walking around, charming everyone in the room. Both men were beaming, yet looked so relaxed and carefree.

"Were you guys as wired as I am when you got married? You look so calm."

"I was wired," Rhett said.

"Me, too," Merit said.

Graham nodded. "But being a groomsman is easier. We're practically pros at it."

Graham and Merit shared a mischievous smile that made him wonder how many couples the two of them had a hand in getting together. He knew that Joy and Thomas had gotten married in the fall, and Addison and Davis had a date set for next summer. Three couples getting married, all because of the same Christmas retreat. And Merit and Graham had been doing the retreat for years.

"When do you leave for this year's retreat?" he asked them.

Merit answered. "Tomorrow morning, bright and early. We are headed to the Royal Palm again, and I can't wait."

"Me, neither," Graham said. "We've got another good group joining us."

Parker chuckled, wondering if any of the people in that group had any idea what they were in for.

He felt a buzz from his phone, so he pulled it out of his pocket and then excused himself from the group. It was a text from Kelli that read, *I'M NERVOUS.*

He typed back, *HAVING SECOND THOUGHTS?*

A year ago, he might've been afraid to ask that question. But now he could ask it, knowing that she would take it as a light-hearted joke. Now he was confident enough in their relationship, and confident enough to know that he always put Kelli first and would know if anything was going off track long before it became a problem.

> KELLI: Haha. Not that kind of nervous.

> Come into the bride's room?

> PARKER: You want me to see you in your wedding dress?

> Isn't that bad luck or something?

But he was already on his way to the bride's room. He'd wanted this wedding to be perfect for Kelli, but, of course, not everything went according to plan. When the flowers arrived, they were missing a boutonniere, several trips had to be made to run back and grab something that was forgotten, one of the tiers on the wedding cake was dropped and practically exploded when it hit the floor, one of the band members got sick, and an entire tray of food was dropped at the rehearsal dinner.

But they pulled together pieces from the other flowers and made another boutonniere, retrieved everything they needed, made the cake look incredible with one less tier, the band found a substitute, they enjoyed the meal served family-style at the rehearsal dinner, and his bride was happy through it all, which was all that mattered.

> KELLI: We already used up all our bad luck.

He was already at the door, knocking.

Valeria opened the door, wearing her pale gold maid of honor gown, smiling. "I'll leave you two alone." Then she turned her head back toward Kelli and said, "I'll be waiting in my spot with your sisters. Don't forget to put that lipstick on before you come out."

Then Valeria walked out the door and Parker stepped into the room to where he could see his bride next to his mother. Kelli stood in front of the full-length mirrors, that smile he loved lighting up her beautiful face and nearly blinding him to anything else. Her hair was a cascade of curls spilling down her back, and her white dress hugged her figure down to her hips before flaring out. She stood tall and confident, shoulders back, looking like a dream come true and quite literally taking his breath away.

His mom turned to Kelli, putting her hands on Kelli's shoulders, and smiled. "Only a few more minutes, and I get a daughter! I'm so happy I'm going to cry!"

"Don't do it," Kelli warned, brushing a fingertip under her eye.

His mom ran a finger under her eye, banishing any threatening tears. "I won't. Okay, I'll leave you two alone. Remember, next time you see me, I'm 'Mom' to you."

The two women hugged, and then his mom gave him a smile before ducking out of the room.

"Wow, Kels. You look incredible."

Her smile was brilliant. The only hint that she was experiencing any nervousness was the way she ran the tip of her thumb over the tips of her first two fingers at her side. In three strides, he was next to her, lifting that hand with his, brushing a kiss across her knuckles. Then he turned her hand slightly and kissed the inside of her wrist. "Tell me what's making you nervous."

She stared at him for a moment, like she'd forgotten her train of thought, and he loved that she still reacted to his touch like that.

Then she glanced toward the door. "I don't know. There are a lot of people out there. I'm afraid I'll trip over my dress and fall or something." She lifted it a bit as if to show that the length and the bulk could be problematic.

"You won't fall. Your dad will be at your side and he has your back—he always does. Besides, even if you trip a little, we still get to be married in less than fifteen minutes."

Her grin was as wide as he was sure that his was. This was really happening. Soon.

"True. The only thing that needs to be perfect is my choice of who to marry. And I'm one hundred percent sure I made the perfect decision."

"I know I did." He closed the gap even more and wrapped his arms around her waist as she reached up and wrapped her arms around his neck. She played with the hair at his neck, and the touch sent even more electricity coursing through his body. As if he hadn't already had more than he knew what to do with. "So how can I help with those nerves?"

A corner of her lip twitched up. "There's a reason why I don't have lipstick on yet."

She pulled him closer to her, and he responded by closing the little bit of space between them, pressing his lips against hers. It didn't matter that they had been together for a year—a kiss from Kelli made his breath catch and his knees weak every single time. He couldn't imagine anything being better than spending the rest of his life with Kelli. The love he felt for her had grown more every single day, filling him to bursting, and he couldn't wait to see what tomorrow brought. Or the next year. Or the next ten years, or fifty, or seventy-five years.

And he would get to spend them all with a woman as amazing as Kelli.

As they kissed, he pulled her closer, their bodies pressed together from their chests nearly down to their feet, and he never wanted to let go.

But then there was a knock at the door just before it opened a bit and Richard poked his head in. "Are you ready, Kelli?"

She pulled back from Parker just enough that he could see her beautiful face and that smile that felt like it was made for him. "As much as I'd like you to stay in here forever, I don't want anything to delay you becoming my husband."

He grinned and gave her one last peck on the lips, then headed toward the door. Right before he walked out, he called back, "Don't forget the lipstick."

"Oh! I nearly did!"

He chuckled.

A few minutes later, he was standing at the altar as his groomsmen walked up the aisle with Valeria as Kelli's maid of honor and her three sisters, whom she had managed to form a pretty tight bond with, as bridesmaids. When they had reached their spots and were facing the guests, the wedding march sounded, and everyone turned as Richard walked Kelli up the aisle.

At one point, Kelli's foot caught on her dress and she faltered just a bit, but her dad held her arm firmly, so it was barely noticeable. She gave Parker a wink, and he knew that no matter how either of them stumbled through their lives, everything would be okay if they had each other.

As she reached the front and he took her hands in his as they looked into each other's eyes, grinning like kids at Christmas, he knew that life was going to be imperfect, but that was okay. They were perfect for each other, and that was all that mattered.

Author's note:

I hope you enjoyed reading Kelli's and Parker's story as much as I enjoyed writing it!

If reading *A Kiss at Christmas* got you in the mood for Christmas romances, check out *The Christmas Pact*. It is filled with loads of chemistry and small-town charm and packed full of Christmas romancey goodness.

You can even get one of my books FREE when you join my newsletter at www.megeaston.com I'll keep you up to date with new releases and other news.

Happy reading!

—Meg

Get the Nestled Hollow series

Coming Home to the Top of Main Street
Second Chance on the Corner of Main Street
Christmas at the End of Main Street
More than Friends in the Middle of Main Street
Love Again at the Heart of Main Street
More than Enemies on the Bridge of Main Street

Listen to the audiobooks on YouTube

About Meg Easton

Meg Easton is the *USA Today* bestselling author of contemporary romances and romantic comedies with fun, memorable, swoon-worthy characters, and settings you'll want to pack up and move to. She lives at the foot of a mountain with her name on it (or at least one letter of her name) in Utah. She loves gardening, bike riding, baking, swimming before the sun rises, and spending time with her husband and three kids.

She can be found online at www.megeaston.com

Sign up to receive her newsletter and stay up to date with new releases, get exclusive bonus content, and more.

If you liked this book please leave a review. Your review can help other readers find books they might fall in love with.

youtube.com/@megeastonauthor

bookbub.com/authors/meg-easton

instagram.com/megeaston_author

facebook.com/MegEastonBooks

tiktok.com/@megeaston_author